To Jack & Jill, warmest
memories..
You're in my first one!

Brian Jarman was born on a farm in Mid-Wales, the joint youngest of five brothers. After studying in London, Paris and Cardiff he joined the South Wales Argus as a reporter and then worked for the BBC for 22 years, mainly as a current affairs editor at The World Service. In 2011 he published his first novel, *The Missing Room.* He's now Senior Lecturer in Journalism at London Metropolitan University.

He would like to thank Annabel Hughes for proof-reading this book, and his niece Rebecca Jarman for her many great ideas.

Love

4 Mar 2014

Reviews for *The Missing Room* BF bold

I loved it. It's a fine novel, very well plotted, full of character, and I couldn't put it down.
Carmen Callil, founder of Virago Press

An ingenious page turner, but with the power to encourage reflection on the human condition - it's all there: family, health, career, and of course the slippery slope to alcoholism.
Clive Jennings, Director of the National Print Gallery

Simply on the strength of a piece of fiction about ME from a male point of view, Jarman deserves five stars. And there is a lot more: the writing is strong, and Mr. Jarman is not only a fine journalist but a great storyteller.
Pamela Post-Ferrante, writer and lecturer

The Fall from Howling Hill

BF

Part One

It must have been taken the summer the Barrys moved into Glanharan. Late summer, just before its glories began to fade and were already tinged with a kind of nostalgia. They'd only been there for the one, of course, as incredible as that now seemed given all that had happened.

The black and white snapshot had been faded to greys by a stiletto of silver light which pierced a corner of the attic where a tile had slipped. Their faces were fuzzy, taken no doubt by the kind of cheap camera that was catching on just then, so it was hard to tell their mood all those years ago. It seemed like a rare moment of calm in those turbulent days, when everyone appeared relaxed, a normal group of people on a sunny Sunday. He could guess what the afternoon had really been like, though. No, not guess - remember, just. The longer he looked the clearer his memory became, itself like a picture fading in reverse – developing, if you will. And he began to taste and smell those far-off days.

They were all lined up against the back of the rambling half-renovated house by the kitchen windows. It was an atypically informal pose, evocative of the days of hefty family albums. The impression was helped by the ghostly shades of the photo, the surprising outward cheeriness of the group. It could almost have been wartime, when such smiling gatherings seemed almost obligatory. But this illusion was shattered by the fashions of the time, the late 1960s. His gaze swept from left to right, lingering on some figures more than others.

Luke was on the left. His dandyish get-up of many colours and long hair which were so with it then – above everything else you had to be with it – now dated him and even imprisoned him in a cliché. He, who had always seemed such an individual, such a character. Everyone said so. Next to him was Sian, so pretty, her shy smile so winning. She was twisting slightly away from Luke, whose face was leaning towards hers. Sian probably came out of it better than anyone - her eyes a little less mascara'd, her skirt a little less mini, her shoulder-length brown hair a little less bouffant than the norms of fashion demanded. Hairspray and mascara were the order of those days. She alone looked natural, timeless. Even Briddy next to her wore a skirt which stopped just sort of her rather podgy knees and looked awkward, as she always did. She never fitted in – maybe that's why everyone loved her. Dear Briddy. Stockton was in the inevitable shirt and tie, but it looked to be one of those flowery, matching sets that were all the rage back then. He was beaming grandly – it could have been a shot of the employee of the month in a company magazine. And then Nia. Nia, with her studied simplicity. She could have worn a pinny, as his mother called an apron, and looked elegant. Her white blouse, flouncy floral skirt and huge glossy buckled belt were at the same time so typical of the era and so

2

artless in their overall effect. Even the standard beehive hairdo looked something of her own creation, thrown together for the photograph.

'No, I'm not ready,' she would have squealed. 'Oh well, you'll have to take me as I am. Wait a minute, will you, while I put two pins in my hair.'

It all seemed so distant, alien, yet familiar. Could he himself have taken the picture? He very much doubted it. He would have remembered. Then who?

It was eerie to find it here in the attic at Glanharan after all these years, half-hidden in a crack in the floorboards. Glyn could imagine the flurry of packing for a hurried flight from the old house, falling out of an album that was being quickly flung into a box or suitcase. Perhaps the packer didn't notice it had fallen out, or else there was no time to pick it up. And here it had lain all this time, waiting to be found, waiting to rekindle painful memories. There was something agonising about holding it in his hand, which he noticed was shaking slightly. But he couldn't put it down. He had to analyse it, search for some kind of meaning, some clues that could shed some light on what was to follow. No, the picture stayed as silent as Nia had been in all the intervening years. Eventually Glyn put it in his pocket, and went back downstairs.

The arrival of the Barrys had been long anticipated in the quiet village of Aberharan, and not always with the greatest of pleasure. In the past his mother had sometimes spoken of Nia Barry, when pressed, with that characteristic little bob of her chin and pursing of her lips which stopped just short of a tut. It acknowledged, perhaps, that such people existed and there was little that could be done about it. But they belonged elsewhere. When it was announced that Nia Barry had bought Glanharan, she blew out a disapproving breath.

Nia Barry was reckoned to have come from up country somewhere with an unspecified, unsavoury past. Up country meant even further up in the hills than Aberharan, which nestled in a little valley at the start of its journey to the sea. Of the years in between these origins and her stardom in Hollywood, little was known, or at least revealed, apart from a handful of second-rate films made in England in the early 1950s. Somewhere along the way, the Sunday papers had informed the locals, she had acquired a son Luke, and later, a husband Carl. Many were scandalised by this tabloid tittle-tattle, but did not seem to pause to consider that they themselves were just as busy circulating the same kind of gossip, and probably even worse.

But others in the village and surrounding areas seemed to like the idea of counting a film star in their number. And that Glanharan was to be rescued from years of dereliction and decay. Glyn, secretly, was among these. He'd finished his A levels the summer before and opted for a year or two off, to work with his two older brothers at Bryngwanwyn before having to decide whether to step outside into the wider world of university and beyond. Maybe having this facet of the wider world move in next door would help with his decision. He knew deep down that life for him was elsewhere. But even though machinery was increasingly replacing manpower on the farm, it was difficult to make the break, or even to discuss it.

Glanharan had been empty for some ten years since Eifion Ellis, headmaster and magistrate, never addressed without a Mister in front, had died childless. Even when it was occupied, the house had been a forbidding place, tucked into a little cleft in the woods half a mile or so below Bryn-

4

gwanwyn. The farm looked over the valley and the village, but Glanharan was facing away, into the higher hills opposite. By road it was a good mile from the farm.

Its red bricks were unusual in this part of Wales, and when the young Glyn braved the shadowy, twisting path down from the farm it was always with a tiny thrill of dread that he first caught sight of its gables through the trees. Then there were still three menaces to face before he reached the house, all on the face of it harmless but requiring courage to pass. First there was the corrugated iron shed down in a dell to the right of the path. There was some mysterious danger within, a bottomless well or maybe a sinister old engine which would start of its own accord for evil purposes.

The path descended on through the woods until it emerged onto a flattened shelf just above the house, where the remains of what his mother had told him were old tennis courts now lurked under grass like an ancient ruin. Glyn would run past it before he could hear the eerie thwack of leather on gut, or whatever made up ball and racket in the old days. And he would always forget that his run would take him to the house too abruptly. He would stumble to a skidding stop above the stables at the back of the house, perilously close to the cobbled back yard. Glanharan had always been the big house of the district, built by the Pryce-Edwards family who'd made their money from wool. As such, it had the aura of a forbidding and forbidden place.

The third test, in his boyhood, was that he had a nameless fear of Mr Ellis which was never calmed by the kind words of his mother, or indeed his own experience of the white-haired old gentleman and his friendly wave. Glyn would run on along the path above Glanharan which led to the Bottom Meadow and the River Haran, looking the other way as if that would protect him.

These feelings dwindled when the old man died and Glyn grew up. But they didn't entirely go away, and the house always held for him some vague dread. Glanharan took on its own ageing life, as stable doors buckled and skewed, the sage-green paint of its windows bubbled and flaked, slates shattered on to the purplish and increasingly grassy cobbles of the back yard by the old stables. It became what Glyn and his brothers called a rack and ruin house. Hopes of finding new owners for the monstrosity vanished. Until now.

Glanharan had been bought the autumn before and the battered sale signs removed. In the New Year a small army of workmen moved in to re-pane the windows and repaint their frames, point the brick and fix the slates, hack the rhododendrons and brambles on the steep bank behind the house, and harvest the hay of the front lawns. Inside, as Glyn passed to feed the sheep on the Bottom Meadow and threw furtive looks through the wide-open front door, he could see cream paint being stripped from the oak stairs and panelling of the hall. Old floorboards, swathes of florid wallpaper and sheets of worn lino were thrown into lorries in the yard. Then came gothic pieces of old furniture, brass bedsteads, a polyphone and an organ. This was accompanied by a symphony of hammers, drills, sanders and cement mixers, drowning the usual sounds of birdsong and spring lambs. Glyn's unseen supervision of this activity as he passed by gave him an odd sense of satisfaction.

Of the new owners there was as yet no sign, but much talk. Every fact and fiction was dredged up by anyone who had the dimmest recollection of Nia Barry, past or present. Small stories about her and her new home appeared in the national press, and bigger ones in the local papers. She was quoted as being overjoyed to be returning to her native soil, not retiring from stage and screen exactly but looking forward to leading a quieter life with her husband and son, leaving the dirt and bustle of New York behind. The stories were usually illustrated by somewhat old-fashioned pictures of the star in her earlier days - publicity shots with pearls and a cigarette holder.

It was rumoured that they would move in around the beginning of June. The topic figured largely in local chit-chat, but Glyn did his best to appear bored with it, or even contemptuous of it. Why he wanted to mask his interest, he couldn't have said.

One Saturday afternoon he was passing by the back of the house with his young nephew and niece, on their way to the Haran to fish with nets. It was a warm but blowy day, with skittish clouds dotting the sky. To Glyn, it was somehow a setting for expectancy, for adventure. As they walked along the path below the woods opposite the back of the house, he saw two Pickfords vans turn in at the deserted front lodge and bounce up the dusty crescent of the drive past newly-mown lawns. Behind them was a sober black Rover containing, he presumed, the Barrys. He stopped and tugged the children into hiding behind some bushes.

'What?' they yelled.

'Shhh,' he whispered, crouching down to their level. 'Look. A film star's moving into the old house.'

He'd had a half-formed vision of a large-finned pastel blue American convertible and whirling white fur. But the woman who stepped out of the passenger seat of the Rover was wearing an ordinary summer dress and headscarf over straggly straw-blond hair. Not even sunglasses. The young man who hopped out of the driver's seat was more to type, with blazer, cravat and a flop of brown hair. They disappeared without ceremony inside the house.

Glyn got up from his crouching position and turned around, but the kids had vanished. He looked up at the woods above them – they were probably playing hide and seek – and then down to the meadow that sloped to the river. Sonia was running full pelt towards it, her net waving wildly. Her brother Hywel, at eight a couple of years older, was jogging a few yards behind her. He was shouting at her to stop, but it was in the spirit of a game. He was unaware of the danger.

Glyn knew that at that precise spot the river's curve had carved away part of the bank, so it was a high drop into the deep water below. At Sonia's height, she would not be able to see this. It would appear that the bank sloped gently down to the water. He didn't know whether or not she could swim, but he very much doubted it – there was no pool for miles around. He bolted down the field, screaming her name. Hywel came to an abrupt halt and turned towards him, then looked back at Sonia to see what she would do. She glanced at him briefly, stumbled, but soon regained her stride and took off, running even faster than before. He heard a squeal of delight. It was a race.

He shouted at Hywel to go after her and the boy set off, uncertain as to what he was meant to do. Glyn continued his sprint, bellowing her name at the top of his lungs. He was gaining ground rapidly, but the knot of agony in his stomach told him he would not reach her in time.

Just then, from the corner of his left eye, he noticed Jack, a neighbouring farmer, ambling along the riverbank with his dog about fifty yards away from Sonia. She herself could only now be a few yards away from the edge.

'Jack!' he shouted. 'Jack! Get her!'

Jack had already spotted the danger and had set off towards the girl, the dog joining in the fun. But Jack was old, and it was clear that with his waddling run he would not make it in time. The only hope now was Hywel. He'd been gaining on her slowly, and finally seemed to realise what he had to do. He was three or four yards away from her, and she was about the same distance from the river.

Then, just as all seemed lost, Sonia came to a shuddering halt, turned around, and laughed at them, her finger in her mouth as if she'd done something very clever.

The three chasers reached her at the same time. Glyn swept her into his arms and hugged her.

'Now, don't ever do that again,' he said. 'You could have fallen into the river, look.'

Sonia's chuckling stopped for a second, and then turned into sobbing. Her triumph had been spoiled.

'Close shave,' said Jack.

'Aye, indeed.'

Glyn led the children upstream to a flat, stony patch where the river consisted of slow-flowing ankle-deep pools. The drama was put behind them as soon as they took off their sandals and paddled in. Sonia and Hywel spent an hour or so splashing about catching, as Glyn expected, nothing. He lay back on the bank, enjoying their busy breeziness with a heightened sense of peace after the crisis. But he knew he'd been at fault – taking his eye of his charges while he was nosing at the arrival of the glamorous new neighbours.

At about half past three they set out to be back at Byngwanwyn in time for tea at four. It was something of a high tea for his brothers before they started the milking. It was part of a strict timetable of meals at the farm. Glyn and his mother, father and grandmother would have a cup, and perhaps a slice of cake. After the milking when his older brother went home, the others would sit down to their meal proper.

As they passed by Glanharan, all was quiet. The Rover stood where it had pulled up, and the vans had gone. They must have been quick at their work, he thought.

They reached the long, low stone farmhouse just in time and as they went in through the back door to the kitchen, chairs were being scraped into position on the flagstone floor around the huge square table covered in oilcloth. The fare barely varied: bread and butter, ham, tomatoes, pickled onions, cheddar cheese, tarts and cake. The children were given shop lemonade, which they called pop.

'Catch anything?' asked their father, Alun, the elder of Glyn's two brothers. Glyn prayed silently – to whom or what he did not know – that the children would say nothing of the misadventure. But it was long-forgotten, and they focussed instead on the many near catches, or misses.

'Anything at Glanharan?' asked his mother, pouring the tea, herself not wanting to display too much curiosity. Glyn told all he had seen.

'Ah well, expect we'll see plenty more before too long, more than we want too, probably,' she said with great resignation, and there was a gentle nodding of assent.

'You went to school with her, didn't you, Mam?' asked Glyn.

'Well, she was a year or two above me,' she said. 'You only really know the ones in your year, don't you?'

'But you knew of her?'

'Couldn't help.'

Glyn could tell by the brevity of his mother's replies that it wasn't something she was keen to talk about, but he pressed on.

'What was she like?'

His mother drew in her breath, as if this were quite a taxing request.

'No better than she ought to have been,' put in his grandmother, moving cake around in her mouth as she didn't have her teeth in.

Glyn had never understood what the phrase meant exactly, nor could he understand why his family all seemed to have already made up their mind about the newcomers. He thought they should be given a chance, at least, although a part of him blamed them for distracting him for that crucial moment. But his mother's attitude served merely to pique further his curiosity and he made up his own mind to be civil to the new neighbours should their paths ever cross.

Glyn changed into his best clothes after supper and set out on his Saturday evening route to the Mucky Duck, as the Black Swan was universally known. This took him, not to the muddy path past Glanharan, but down the farm lane and then a mile or two on the main road to the edge of Aberharan.

The bar was a mix of authentic oak beams and settles, and replica horse brasses and red Formica on the bar. In the middle of this a patch had worn through its red and white layers to the brown, where change was chucked and scooped. It was fringed with cigarette burns. The usual crowd was there, a handful of people near Glyn's age and the rest older, mainly farmers. He was given a pint of Red Dragon without asking, and put one in for his friend Johnny Jones, invariably known by both names, who was leaning on his left elbow against the bar with the air of one at home. They soon got down to chewing over the business of the day, their conversation low and sparse at this early stage of the night. Others around the bar chipped in from time to time - lamb prices, a local football match, the latest idiocies of the government and alcoholic excesses of common acquaintances. Two young men sat on stools at the bar talking about someone Glyn tried in vain to identify.

'I never knew he drank till I met him sober,' said one to the other.

It was a restorative, comfortable rite, carried out with an almost military sense of pack drill and duty.

Sometime after eight the door was thrust open with far more than the customary force, so that the tinkle of the latch and measured creak became more of a rattle and a screech. Glyn recognised the driver of the Rover at Glanharan, wearing the same outlandish outfit. He would be three or four years older than Glyn, but his whole mien spoke of someone altogether more mature. He strode confidently over to the bar, bestowing little nods and grins as he went.

'Hullo, Landlord,' he said loudly, lighting a cigarette 'Brace of Grouse, please.'

'Beg pardon?' said Ed, pausing his vigorous glass polishing. He tilted his head to the side and frowned. Could this newcomer be mistaking his premises for a poacher's clearing house?

'Large Grouse. One lump of ice.'

As Ed reached for the optic the murmur of conversation died out altogether, apart from Dai in the corner. He was talking to himself but his speech was so slurred people could hardly tell whether he was speaking English or Welsh. The rest of the locals took in this exotic creature with a mix of interest, suspicion and embarrassment.

'Well, well, here we are then,' said the stranger after he had gulped down a good half of his glass. He leant on the bar with one elbow, clearly oblivious to the atmosphere his entrance had created. His eyes swept the room and came to rest on Glyn and Johnny Jones. 'What does one do for entertainment in these parts?'

'I'll have another,' said an old man hunched over the end of the bar, firmly reverting to the business in hand. A trio at a nearby table switched to Welsh to discuss the young man freely. Their opinions were not favourable.

'You from Glanharan?' enquired Johnny Jones, winking at Glyn.

'Yes. Luke Harrington,' and he held out his hand. Johnny Jones and Glyn shook it warily.

'So aren't you Nia Barry's son then?'

'Oh. Yes, I am,' said Luke. He seemed unused to having to explain. 'That's her stage name. Sort of. My father's dead. We think.'

The information was received in silence and Luke seemed to feel that more was required.

'She remarried. And my stepfather's name is something different altogether.'

For the taciturn assembly around the bar, unaccustomed to such complicated arrangements, this amounted to full-scale autobiography. It was difficult to know how to respond to such a gush.

'There we are then. Johnny Jones,' said Johnny Jones, raising his pint pot. 'Glyn,' he said, nodding at Glyn.

'Charmed,' said Luke. This provoked a snort and a snigger from within the crowd. Glyn wondered if he'd already had a drink or two.

'Are you moving in there, yourself then?' he asked.

14

'Well, yes. Just down from Oxford. Until I figure out what to do. Ma's here full time. Stockton works a lot of the time in London and the States but he'll come when he can. Her husband. He's a producer.'

'What does he produce?' asked Johnny Jones.

The stranger looked at him warily, as if it were a trick question.

'Films,' he said, with a slight question mark in his voice.

His audience remained determinedly unimpressed, and there was more silence.

'And there's Briddy, of course. She'll be down here a lot of the time too, no doubt. She's her......sort of companion. And the whole crowd'll come and go, I suppose.'

He looked around the bar rather shiftily, as if he was boring himself.

'There we are then,' said Johnny Jones again, deciding that was all the information he needed for now. And as the novelty of Luke wore off a little, the hum grew gently again. The odd comment and scowl of suspicion were aimed his way, but he seemed not to notice.

'Village idiot?' enquired Luke, nodding towards Dai.

'No,' said Johnny Jones, 'he failed the exam,' and they exchanged sly smiles.

Johnny Jones chatted away with him amicably enough, although Glyn could tell that he wished Luke wasn't quite so brash. He gave him a beginner's guide to the area and his ways, its attractions and pitfalls. He worked in the bank in Aberharan and travelled around to other branches in his large constituency, as he called it.

'Know this part of Wales well, do you?' he asked, as Luke appeared bewildered by much he said.

'First time,' admitted Luke with raised eyebrows and the breath of a laugh.

'Ah. Here, have an Embassy,' said Johnny Jones, throwing the cigarette at him.

'Where are all the chicks?' asked Luke, lighting it with a flourish.

'The dancing girls come on later,' said Johnny Jones.

'Really?'

'No. Not really. You'll have to make do with me and Glyn here for the time being.'

Luke looked crestfallen for a moment, but soon recovered and settled down into the business of the banter. It must have been around ten when the door burst opened again and Micky Lewis and his sidekicks staggered in. They would have been at the match and made a day of it, crawling around all five of Aberharan's pubs and ending up at the Mucky Duck which was usually far too tame for them. Any trouble, it was said, and you could bet your bottom dollar that Micky Lewis was behind it.

Luke glanced at them in a bored, annoyed kind of way and plunged back into his latest story. Micky swaggered to the bar and ordered a round. Ed sized him up for a moment and decided to give them the benefit of the doubt. Micky swigged back half a pint as the others were being poured, swung unsteadily around to see who was about, spotted Luke for the first time and immediately saw some sport. He lurched next to him, clutching at the bar and jostling quite a lot of Grouse from his glass.

'Sorry,' bellowed Micky provocatively into Luke's face, blowing a wisp of foam from his upper lip.

'Quite alright,' mumbled Luke.

'Quaite awlrait? What are ya, some kind of fucking fairy?'

'Barking up the wrong tree there, I'm afraid,' said Luke in conversational tones, and drew on his cigarette with one eye closed.

'I'll give yo wrong bleeding tree,' and Micky swung for him, catching him square on the lip.

'Right, that's it. Finish your drink and be off,' said Ed. 'I've told you before I don't want no trouble here and if you don't clear out I'll be talking to the other landlords in the town and it'll be a total ban.'

Micky stared at Ed weighing things up a moment and said, 'Aw, you're not fucking worth it.'

He grabbed Luke by his cravat. 'And you,' he growled between gritted teeth, 'I'll be seeing you around' and pushed him roughly back. 'C'mon,' he said to his gang, waiting to see if there was a fight on. 'Who wants to be in a fucking crud-hole like this anyway?' and off he slouched, kicking a stool out of his way, seeing his gang out while staring unsteadily at Luke, and slamming the door.

'What did I do?' asked Luke, dabbing a huge red hanky to his bleeding lip.

'Don't take any notice of him,' said Johnny Jones. 'He's trouble. It's just a sort of initiation ceremony. And you do sound funny,' he added, trying to be helpful. 'Have another Grouse.'

'Are all the locals as friendly as that?'

Glyn found himself admiring the cool way Luke had handled himself. Cool hand Luke. Or was it just bravado? He said as much, implying that the stranger had done well to hide his fear.

'Good Lord, no. Why would I be scared of a little tyke like that?'

'He stabbed his mother.'

'Stabbed his mother? Then why on earth is he still wandering the streets? You do have streets here, don't you?'

Good point, thought Glyn. It was one of those things the locals always said, so everyone was more than a little wary of Micky Lewis. But come to think of it, it was probably just a rural myth. The incident served to forge a strange bond between the three, though, and in a way each of the three were surprised how easily they got on, given how little they had in common. Luke seemed to enjoy the banter, and gave as good as he got, which was the main thing. At closing time, they found themselves the last three in the bar after a short lock-in. Finally Ed draped the tea towels over the pumps and said it was time to call it a night. The three lingered outside and had a last cigarette. They'd all had a good drink but suddenly the pub glow seemed to wear off, leaving them strangely tongue-tied and unsure of how to bring the evening to an end. Stubbing out his fag end, Johnny Jones waved them a cheery if somewhat wobbly goodnight and made his way up the dark road.

'Where are you off now?' asked Luke of Glyn.

'Home,' said Glyn.

'Where's that?'

'The farm on the hill above your place.'

'Give you a ride if you like?' said Luke, swaying slightly.

'No, you're alright,' said Glyn. He usually got a lift with his brother, who went drinking in a pub further down the valley. 'Anyway, do you think you're in any fit state?'

'Why, do you have breathalysers in these parts? PC Plod going to come along on his bike and stop me?'

'Well, be careful. They do stop people at this time of night, especially strange cars.'

'Huh. We'll soon see about that,' said Luke, lurching for the door of the Rover. 'Anyway, see you around – next Saturday, maybe?'

'Maybe.'

A week later Glyn was standing in the same spot at the bar, listening to variations on a theme. Johnny Jones was taking his girlfriend to the pictures in Aberystwyth. It had been a busy week harvesting the barley and Glyn was ready for a good drink. He'd seen no more of the Glanharan newcomers. At idle moments he'd wondered if Luke and the Rover had made it home in one piece. The evening before he'd passed by the house. A delivery van and a decorator's pick-up with ladders and dust-sheets in the back were parked in the yard alongside the big black car which seemed unscathed. There was no sign of life, but muted sounds of it within. Glyn had also wondered vaguely how much, if at all, the Barrys intended to mix with the locals. Perhaps last Saturday's encounter would dampen what little enthusiasm they had had.

But not long after eight, the door was thrust open with the same brashness, and in breezed Luke wearing yet again, Glyn could have sworn, the same rig-out.

'Lo, there,' said Glyn.

'Hullo. Glyn, isn't it? Can I fill her up?'

And without waiting for an answer to either question he turned to Ed.

'Brace of Grouse, one lump, and a pint in there,' pre-empted Ed.

'Marvellous,' said Luke, and when he'd paid for the drinks, Luke nodded to an empty table in the alcove by the window.

'Shall we?' he enquired of Glyn, who followed him to the seats even though it was somewhat irregular to move away from the bar this early on in the evening. The local crowd still regarded Luke with a subdued wariness but were already paying him less attention than the week before. He gave a loud groan of satisfaction as he sat down and positioned himself at the table as a committee chairman might when calling proceedings to order.

'Down to business then. I think I told you about me last Saturday. Can't remember you volunteering much information. What do you get up to?'

'I live at the farm above your new house,' said Glyn, remembering he'd said this last Saturday.

'What's it called?'

'Bryngwanwyn.'

'Bring-what-in?'

'Brin-gwan-win. It means Spring Hill.'

'Does it, now,' mused Luke, as if only just registering that there was a wholly separate language. 'So you speak the lingo?'

'I get by,' said Glyn, who did not at this moment want to go into the rather complicated linguistic patterns in his family. He had not yet made his mind up about Luke, although he had to admire his panache.

'What does Glanharan mean then?'

'On the banks of the Haran.'

'Hmm. You certainly pack a lot into three syllables. So what do you do on Spring Hill?'

Glyn outlined the work he did with his brothers - the milking, lambing, harvesting and so on, feeling decidedly dull compared to the life Luke must have lived. Although Luke seemed quite interested in all this, as if learning about an exotic culture, Glyn felt compelled to explain that he was still exploring options.

'The way things are going, we're not sure it'll support all three of us. So I have to think about going away - maybe to University.'

'Well, don't you want to?'

'I'm not sure.'

'What would you study?'

'English, maybe.'

'Well, I'd highly recommend Uni. It's got lots going for it. Plenty of chicks, and the work doesn't get in the way too much. That means we're in more or less the same boat. I've decided to take the summer off. Without worrying about what to do next. Plenty of time for that. So we can have fun in the next few months.'

'I have to work,' said Glyn.

'Oh, even farmers have time off, surely. We can always squeeze in fun. Talking of which, where does one find entertainment round here?'

'Well there's Owen Pantheulog over there,' said Glyn with a smile, nodding at the grinning raconteur holding court on the settle by the fireplace. 'He's always good for a tale or two.'

Luke gave Glyn an appraising nod, as if just realising that he had a sense of humour. Johnny Jones had made most of the running the week before.

'What a strange name,' he said.

'It's the name of his farm really. I mean Pantheulog.'

'You mean you call people by where they live?'

21

'Yes, with farmers you usually do,' said Glyn, thinking for a moment. 'Sometimes it's after their job. Like Will Post. The postman,' he added, seeing Luke didn't quite get it. 'Or Dai Chalk.'

'The teacher,' they said together, and laughed.

'I thought that was just a parody. A joke,' said Luke.

'No, it's what people say.'

'So you're Glyn Brynthingammyjig?'

'Bryngwanwyn. No, not really - it would be a bit of a mouthful, wouldn't it?'

'How long before I'll be Luke Glanharan?'

'Oh, I don't think you'll ever be Luke Glanharan,' said Glyn with a chuckle, and Luke looked disappointed.

'Well, anyway, what I meant by entertainment was the sexual variety. You look like someone who could handle yourself with the opposite sex.'

'Oh, well, there are other pubs, dances, village shows..........'

'Stop, stop, this is all getting too much,' and without asking he stuck his cigarette in the corner of his mouth, closed one eye against the smoke, and scooped up the glasses.

'My round,' said Glyn, standing up quickly.

'Look sharp then,' smiled Luke, surrendering the glasses. 'A boy could die of thirst'.

And so the two passed the evening, little by little finding out more about their distant worlds. A couple of Glyn's friends walked in after nine, but Luke was in flow so all Glyn could do was wave rather sheepishly. He was intrigued by the newcomer, and he was undoubtedly entertaining. But he was wary of forming too close a friendship, as Luke seemed keen to do. There was the mysterious hostility of his family towards Luke's mother, for one thing, although if anything this merely served to pique Glyn's curiosity. Then there was the antipathy of the locals to this foppish Englishman, for that is how they saw him. Even though he had been born in America, he'd spent much of his youth in boarding schools in England. The English were not always popular with the people of this remote and somewhat isolated part of Wales, and while their antagonism did not on the whole reach the extremes of Micky Lewis and his ilk, they did not bother to hide their disapproval. Again, though, this irked Glyn and a baulky streak in his nature meant he'd be damned if he was going to let it influence him.

When Ed rang time, Luke lit one last cigarette and said, 'So this is your usual haunt then, of a Saturday evening.'

'Yeah.'

'Perhaps I'll see you here next week?'

'Perhaps. So long'

When he got home his mother was sleeping in front of the TV in the kitchen but woke instantly on hearing the door. Her last job of the day was to make his father's coffee when he got in from his local and she set about busying herself at the sink.

'Good night?' she asked.

'Alright. Got talking to the Glanharan boy.'

'Ooooh,' she said in a slight sing-song which denoted something out of the ordinary. 'Bit of a peacock by all accounts.'

'He's alright.'

'Well let's hope he's better than that mother of his.'

'And what's wrong with her exactly? You never say.'

'Probably more than I could tell you.'

The rumble of the old Land Rover outside announced the arrival of his father, and the fumbling with the latch signalled, if signal were needed, that he was slightly the worse for wear.

'Aaaah,' he grunted as he fell into the worn old leather armchair by the range, expressing in one long syllable greeting, satisfaction with his evening and pleasure at being home.

'He's been drinking with Nia Barry's boy,' said his mother as she plonked his father's cup and saucer – never a mug – on the range with a clatter.

'Oh aye?' said his father, but he couldn't have looked less interested. She looked annoyed with him, as if he had failed to back her up in some way.

Glyn made up his mind to get to the bottom of her animosity to the Barrys, to Nia anyway. To disapprove was one thing, but it was another to knock her at every opportunity, and it was unlike his mother, who usually tried to see some good in everybody. But it wasn't going to be easy.

3

Glyn gave the Mucky Duck a miss the next Saturday, for no particular reason that he could put into words, or indeed thoughts. He was still a little wary of his new friend, if that's what he was, perhaps not wanting in the local way to commit to too much too early. Despite himself, he still had had qualms that he would find Luke embarrassing if he didn't keep his distance. But he was also determined not to give way to the prejudices of the locals and did his best to stifle such thoughts.

Late the next Wednesday afternoon he was on his way back from the Bottom Meadow where he'd been sorting out some sheep. It was shaping up to be a glorious summer; 'a summer like we used to have' was the phrase on everyone's lips. 'The kind of summer where you could hang up your coat in May and not take it down again until September,' was how his mother described it, and added, 'apart from the odd thunderstorm'. These summers seemed largely to have died out after the War.

As he trundled up the path behind Glanharan, Glyn spotted Luke lounging on a sun bed in the yard reading a book through dark glasses and sipping a heavily-iced drink through a straw. He was wearing canvas shorts
and an old fashioned straw hat and his body already had the even tan of
holiday brochures.

'Hi there,' called Luke enthusiastically, but without stirring from his position. 'Didn't see you in the Swan at the weekend.'

Glyn ambled over more out of politeness than anything else and planted
himself a conversational distance away, his hands on hips, looking around.
The back door was open, but all was quiet.

'Nah. Something else on.'

'Ha! I knew I was right about you and the ladies. I did look in there and
chatted with a couple of the old fogeys for an hour or two. Quite interesting when they get going. I think they're getting a little more used to me
now,' he said with a slight self-deprecating smile. 'Pimm's?' he offered,
holding up his glass.

'What's that?'

'Pimm's. Essential summer drinking.'

'Better not. On my way home for tea,' he said, and then realised with vex-
ation how rustic he sounded. And looked.

'Don't let me stop you. I just thought we could get together for an outing
soon. So you could introduce me to some of the natives. Of the dancing
variety. I did hear there's a village dance nearby somewhere on Saturday.'

'Llanfair. After the show.'

'Show? Broadway comes to The Cambrian mountains?'

'Village show, sort of farm things.'

'Mmm, I know what sort of farm things I'll be after. 'Bout time I met a few dairy maids. I could do with a roll in the hay. What say we go together? I could soup up the old Rover here and we could arrive in style. I hear it's fancy dress. They *are* pushing the boat out, aren't they?'

'A lot of them do, but I'm not,' said Glyn, recognising a little too late that he was entering into a pact. He would usually go to one of the local dances with Johnny Jones and their circle. What would they think if he went with Luke?

'Won't we look out of place?' asked Luke, neatly sealing it. You probably won't, thought Glyn, but he said, 'You can wear whatever you like.'

'That's settled then. Shall I pick you up around seven?'

'No. I'll wait for you at the bottom of your lane.'

'Fine.'

'So long then,' said Glyn and started up the path.

'So long,' Luke shouted after him. 'Oh, and Glyn.'

'What?' threw Glyn back over his shoulder.

'Do practise sentences of more than three words between now and then. The women like a bit of banter.'

And Glyn continued on his way, grinning to himself.

Come Saturday, and Glyn found himself secretly looking forward in a way to the dance. He even had a brief moment of regret at foregoing the fancy dress. He didn't know why he'd told Luke he wasn't bothering. It was something of a local tradition for high days and holidays. He told himself that Luke and fancy dress would be a little too much in one evening. But maybe, in a way, it would have been better.....

'Going to Llanfair dance?' asked his mother, clattering away the tea things.

'Thought I might.'

'Got your costume?'

'Not bothering.'

'Plenty of people around, anyway,' said his father from his armchair. He'd been to the show that afternoon with the eldest son and his family.

'Ydy e'n mynd gyda Johnny Jones?' asked his Nain, bent over the sink washing up. His grandmother preferred to speak Welsh to his mother, and would often ask her questions about other people in the room, as if through an interpreter. This practice was often seen as a ploy to annoy his father, who spoke no more than a handful of Welsh words. And if it was, it was a successful one.

'No, I'm going with the Glanharan boy, Nain,' said Glyn, answering for himself in English.

'Well he won't have to dress up, will he?' said his mother with one of her chuckles to herself.

'Mam, don't be so narrow-minded.' He'd thought the same thing himself, of course.

His mother merely grunted.

Glyn arrived at the Glanharan gates promptly. He had a good sense of timing and the walk down the road - he didn't want to soil his shoes on the path - had taken the eighteen minutes he had allowed. He'd somehow thought he might be in for a wait, but as he arrived he saw the Rover charge down the drive trailing a wake of dust. Luke crunched the car to a halt and told him to hop in.

He was wea·ing a burgundy velvet jacket, a collarless white shirt and pale green and white striped trousers which could easily be mistaken for pyjamas.

'I know what you're thinking,' said Luke with a smirk as they sped off. 'I'm not meant to be anything. Just myself. Glad to see you've made the effort.'

Glyn's jeans, checked shirt and leather jacket were pretty ordinary, he knew. Perhaps that was the way he wanted it.

'You've got to have a few feathers to catch the chicks, you know,' said Luke.

'I dunno. Round here they seem to laugh at anything different.'

'Oh, that's just a cover. They'll be looking at me from the corner of their eyes, you'll see.'

They won't bother with the corners, thought Glyn.

The dance was in Llanfair village hall, which Luke seemed surprised to find was a very modern affair, with a vast sloping roof and tall narrow single panes of glass. Set among the pines on the hill above the town, it had a Nordic aspect.

Proceedings were already in full swing as they went in. Inhibitions had already been shed in the beer tent that afternoon, and there was an array of striking costumes. The rugby team was in drag, including a set of Three Degrees.

'Lord, I expected it to be full of tarts and vicars,' said Luke.

'There probably are a few, but they'll be in costume,' said Glyn.

'Ha! Tally-ho,' said Luke, and he plunged towards the bar, shouting 'Gangway, girls,' to a troop of St Trinians and producing a trail of giggles and facetious remarks.

Glyn could see people looking Luke up and down, trying to make out what he was.

Johnny Jones, his girlfriend and another young couple were congregated near the bar, and Glyn hung back to say hello.

'Oh, there you are,' he said to Glyn. 'Thought you'd ring me for a lift in the Land Rover.'

'Well, he was pretty anxious for me to come up with him. Must be a bit lonely not knowing anyone here.'

'Up to you, boy,' said Johnny Jones cheerfully. He was a good friend, with an easy going and sociable manner.

Luke came up with a couple of pints.

'Shall we?' he said to the group when he realised that introductions would not be forthcoming, and nodded to an empty table. The girls smiled at each other in surprise and made a move to go. The boys hung back.

'We usually stand around here for a bit,' said the other friend.

'Nonsense,' said Luke. 'You get a better vantage point in a good seat, with your lap at the ready.' He was already leading the way, plonking himself down and wasting no time in getting down to the business of surveying gyrating gypsies and witches.

'She'd be alright if you did her up a bit,' he shouted in a whisper to Glyn above the noise of the disco after a while. He nodded to a girl standing at the edge of the dance floor with her friend, neither of them dressed up. Glyn looked a little taken aback.

'Don't you like your women with a bit of slap on them?' asked Luke.

'I guess we're more used to taking them as they come.'

'Surely you don't mean to tell me that feminism has reached Wild Wales. I thought women were still down for fetching and carrying in these parts.'

'They can muck in with the rest of them when there's work to be done,' said Glyn. 'It's only in the cities you have bosses and secretaries and that kind of thing.'

The group found it difficult to talk, partly because of the noise, and partly, thought Glyn, because of this exotic stranger who'd thrown them off their stride. But Luke couldn't sit still for very long. He was soon off scouting for partners. The couples had one or two dances and Glyn let himself be dragged up by some of the girls he knew. He was not much of a dancer. He felt awkward and self-conscious. From time to time he caught Luke spinning some line to a partner who clearly didn't know what to make of him, something about a rock band in London and a single about to be released.

Luke would come back at intervals to give Glyn updates on his latest conquests. He was very taken with one, and he pointed her out, sitting on a bar stool with a couple of friends, her face illuminated by the lights behind the bar. She was a little older than most of the others, probably in her early thirties. She was indeed striking. She had shinning brown shoulder-length hair and a rich, natural colour on her high cheeks. She had a pleasant, amused look on her face but there was something aloof, enigmatic about her. Maybe that's what Luke found so alluring, a certain inaccessibility. She hadn't succumbed to his easy charms. She was dressed as Emma Peel from The Avengers, in black from head to foot including knee-length leather boots.

Bit by bit Luke charmed the others into good-natured banter. They were soon laughing with him more than at him. Glyn couldn't help but admire his social abilities, and even though he probably wouldn't have admitted it to himself, he tried surreptitiously to pick up a couple of pointers.

Emma Peel, though, remained elusive. Luke sauntered past her a couple of times, and Glyn could see him trying to engage her in conversation, but she obviously gave him short shrift, although the rather mischievous smile still played on her lips.

At quarter past eleven the grill came down on the bar and the DJ spun his last. The crowd thinned out but Glyn's group lingered, finishing their drinks. It had been a good evening in the end. Luke had won them over, and Glyn was pleased, although it wasn't exactly the relaxing time they would have had without him. The atmosphere was like the crackle after a record had finished: they wanted to relish the evening a little before they acknowledged it was over.

As they were leaving Luke looked round for Emma Peel but she'd disappeared. He asked Glyn if he knew her, and Glyn said no, although was there something vaguely familiar about her?

As they all walked out to the car park, Glyn realised that Luke was in quite a state. He was swaying from side to side. But he wouldn't hear of Glyn driving, and waved aside Johnny Jones's offer to take them all back and bring Luke to fetch his car the next day. Luke was quite a handful. Johnny Jones looked at Glyn, raised his eyebrows and nodded towards his Land Rover, as if to say he'd drive him back home and leave Luke to fend for himself. Glyn didn't feel he could abandon Luke, but he was worried about how he would manage on the unfamiliar country lanes. The breathalyser had not long been introduced, and while it was widely ridiculed and ignored, there was such a thing as tempting fate, thought Glyn. He got in the car reluctantly, wondering if he'd be getting out the right way up.

The worry proved well-founded. Luke raced off, screeching and careering round corners and hogging the middle of the road when it straightened out a little. And a couple of times he came perilously close to the nearside edge, where Glyn knew there to be a deep drop. But although Luke drove too fast, he did drive quite well, and seemed to sober up remarkably quickly in the night air that came whooshing through the window. Glyn let out a sigh of relief when they reached the village.

'Want to come back for a nightcap?' asked Luke as they approached Glanharan.

'No, ta. Better be getting back.'

Luke insisted on driving Glyn up to the farm.

'Will you find your way back?' asked Glyn, leaning over the car door outside the farmhouse. 'Down the lane, right at the bottom, over the bridge, right at the T-junction, and the Glanharan gates are about a quarter of a mile. Got that?'

Luke leaned towards him slightly.

'Look, thanks for coming with me. I know you'd probably prefer to have gone with your mates. You did me a kindness.'

Glyn smiled, and did not feel the need to protest.

'I think it's about time you met Ma,' said Luke, adopting a more businesslike tone. 'You'll have to sooner or later. I suppose you'll be having your farm tea tomorrow afternoon?'

'Well, all the family come on Sundays. I'd better be there.'

'Come after. At six. For cocktails. I insist.'

'Alright then. Thanks for the lift.'

Glyn slammed the door, and smiled as he went up the back door steps. It was hard not to like Luke, and yet there was something he couldn't quite put his finger on that was warning him not to get too close.

4

Sunday tea at Bryngwanwyn was the weekly gathering of the clan, subject to subtle, unspoken regulations. There had to be a clear reason for not attending. Glyn's oldest brother Alun came with his wife and two children from their cottage a couple of miles away. His middle brother Tom was courting a local girl and didn't spend much time at home, but he was expected to be there on Sunday afternoon.

It took place on the large, scrubbed wooden table in the kitchen and the whole family squeezed on the settle on the wall side and the bench on the other side, with his mother and father occupying either end on carver chairs. It wasn't exactly a family council to discuss great issues, but anything of importance generally got a laconic airing.

It was a typically old-fashioned high tea, unceremonious but abundant, with ham, cold chicken, tomatoes, cucumber and spring onions, cheese and pickles, fruit tarts, sponge cake and – something of a Sunday treat because it was bought from a shop - Battenberg. This was known as window cake because its squares resembled panes.

Glyn sat on the bench with his niece and nephew, nervously wondering how to announce his invitation to Glanharan and the fact that he would not be helping with the milking.

'Bolting it down a bit, artn't thee?' said his mother. 'Got a train to catch?'

'A man that's quick at his food.....,' began his father, and paused, looking at the youngest They took their cue and finished off '......is quick at his work,' in a mechanical, bored sort of way.

'As a matter of fact, I've been invited down to Glanharan.'

This piece of news was digested in silence for a moment or two.

'What for?' asked his mother.

'Well, drinks.'

'We've got drinks here,' said his mother.

'Joining the cocktail set now are we, Glyn boy?' said his oldest brother. 'You watch out - it'll be drugs and wild orgies before you know where you are.'

'Alun!' warned his wife, nodding at the children who seemed not to be listening but were unusually quiet.

Glyn never thought of his family as that good at communicating, but it was remarkable how they could come to a collective view of something without exchanging more than a couple of words on the matter. Drinks at Glanharan were clearly seen as dangerously decadent. His mother got up and began clearing away the things.

'No, I'll do it Nain,' she said as the old woman struggled to get out from her corner of the settle. 'You sit down and enjoy your tea.'

Glyn could tell from the way she clattered the dishes in the sink that she was annoyed. On his way out of the back door he glanced to see if she would look up and say anything. She washed grimly on. As he passed by the open window, he looked in at her.

'You don't like me having anything to do with Glanharan, do you?'

'Oh, it's up to you what you do, I'm sure.'

'But you don't approve, do you?'

'There's probably better ways you could spend your time,' she said, scrubbing a pan with particular vigour.

'I'm just going to have a look, Mam. The boy's alright. Just being a good neighbour,' he said, trying a weak smile.

'Oh, you're old enough to decide for yourself. It's not for me to tell you who to like and who to not.'

Glyn thought that's exactly what she was trying to do, in her own way.

'You should be glad I'm mixing.'

She looked at him.

'You can't tell other people what to feel, Glyn. Your feelings are your own,' and turned back into the room to get on with the clearing up.

It was a splendid summer's evening as Glyn walked down the path to Glanharan, its long shadows highlighting the vivid colours with which the sinking sun washed the countryside. In the distance the waves of hills got bluer and greyer and there was a whiff of wood smoke in the air. He played back his mother's comments in his mind. He knew she was torn about him leaving the farm and going to university. She wanted him to do well, knew there wasn't another good living to be had from the farm and that increasing mechanisation meant there would be less and less scope in the future. Yet she didn't want him to go away. All this had been hinted at but never fully discussed. But maybe she was now resigned to the fact that he would have to leave, and was worried that mixing with these undesirables – for that's what they undoubtedly were in her eyes – would make him want to stay for the wrong reasons.

When he came to the back door of the big house it was open and there was a stillness about the place. He peered into the long dark back corridor that opened into various rooms - a scullery, a butler's pantry, the kitchen - and then led into the rather grand wooden-panelled front hall. He called out, but there was no response. He crept in, almost on tiptoe, which was rather daft as he wanted to draw attention to his presence. He called out again, louder.

'Hello-oh?'

'In here,' came a muffled voice from a room off to the right behind the scullery. Glyn continued his slow, quiet walk into the huge kitchen which was a curious mix of old and new, the huge black range bearing gleaming copper pots and the built-in Welsh dresser beside it displaying large, plain white plates.

A woman come out of a large and evidently well-stocked pantry holding a cocktail glass of clear liquid with a pickled onion in it. At the same time Luke bounded up the passage.

'There you are. Oh, Ma, you haven't started already?'

'Just a little one to practise the mix,' with the grin of a naughty child. She looked at Glyn as if deciding whether or not he would be her friend.

'Hello, I'm Nia,' she said holding out her hand to Glyn. 'And as Luke is so dire at introductions I must summon all my powers of intuition and deduce that you are Glyn. I've heard so much about you. Truth be told I was a little nervous of meeting you and was just having a little fortifier. Won't you join me in a Martini? I mix a mean one. You can say a lot about me, but never knock my Martinis. They're just divine. How do you like yours?'

She took a huge swig from the glass in her hand. She was wearing a low-cut black dress and a string of pearls. Her thick straw-coloured hair was sculpted severely at the back and a little straggly in the front. Her voice was warm and husky with a slight edge to it. Her accent held a trace of something familiar to Glyn, but it was tempered by her trained diction and some very slight American tinges. She'd kept her figure and a lot of her beauty. Time and lotion had been good to Nia Barry. Her face suggested intelligence, kindness, humour and strength.

Glyn was still marvelling that anyone, let alone a film star, could be nervous of meeting him, and pondering how to order his Martini, beyond shaken or stirred. Nia was waiting for an answer.

'Oh, however you like them.'

'Correct response. Vodka dry, straight up, shaken with an onion. Same for you darling?' she enquired of Luke while setting to with the shaker. 'I have my own little bar here in the pantry for those quiet moments when ceremony is not called for.'

She handed them their glasses and chinked Glyn's with hers.

'Here's how,' she said, knocking hers back. 'Now let's go and join the others.'

'I'm afraid I didn't dress up,' said Glyn, looking down at his scruffy jeans.

'How very sensible of you. Everything's becoming so much more casual these days, isn't it?'

She slipped her free arm through Glyn's and walked him down to the living room with Luke trailing behind. No-one could have done more to put him at his ease and some of his nerves were already beginning to wear off.

The room was not like one Glyn had ever seen before, and he had to stop himself from gawping too much. It seemed all white and cream, with bed-sized sofas on the polished oak floor, the huge windows bare apart from the parchment-coloured pull-down shades. It contained easily the largest amount of lamps Glyn had ever seen in one place. Slabs of Modern Art filled the walls, and through the arch a huge glass dining table bore an enormous vase of flowers.

'This is the one room I'm quite pleased with,' said Nia, noting Glyn's furtive appraisal. 'We've still got so much to do to the rest of the house. Now, introductions - Luke take note. This is my husband Stockton who spends a lot of his time in the States so we don't have to put up with him very much, and this is my dear friend Briddy whom I've known for decades since the early London days. This is Glyn Bennett from the farm up the hill.'

Glyn nodded and got a firm handshake and 'Howdya do' from the portly Stockton and a smile and 'Hello' from the small and distinctly unglamorous Briddy. Somehow though she oozed charm and grace. She was the first black person Glyn had met. He smiled, wondering whether to be extra nice to her, or if that would be wrong.

'Splendid. Now let's all sit down and get to know each other.'

They sank into the vast cream sofas which flanked the glass coffee table: Briddy, Nia and Stockton on one side and Luke and Glyn the other. Glyn looked out of the windows at the sweeping views across the Haran valley to the hills the other side, to where cows were plodding into the fields after milking. For the first time in his life, he had the sense of looking in on his own world from far away. It was a cosy, warm world, but this new one was exciting.

'I always think that the light is different in Wales from anywhere else in the world,' said Nia, seeing Glyn looking out to the mountains the other side. 'Especially on a Sunday. There's always something different about Sunday weather, isn't there? There's something peaceful about it, and when the sun shines it's more golden. Do you think that could be why it's called Sunday? There's proper weather here, as my Gran used to say. Although I'm almost positive she never saw anywhere else's weather in her entire life. Just look at the glow on those hills.'

'What are they called, those hills?' asked Stockton. His voice was such a boom that Glyn almost jumped.

'Well, that big one just opposite is called The Bryn,' said Glyn.

'And what does that mean?'

'The Hill,' said Glyn, with a shrug. Stockton and Luke laughed. Glyn wondered whether they thought he was being funny or stupid, but decided to settle for a compliment.

'It's true,' said Nia. 'Welsh can be very straightforward.'

'What about that funny shaped one behind it?' said Stockton, his face still wearing a look of amusement.

'That's called Bryn Grwnan.' said Glyn. 'Humming Hill, I suppose you'd say in English. But it's a bit more than humming - howling perhaps.'

'So it is,' said Nia, nodding, as if remembering. 'Isn't it something to do with the noise the wind makes as it whistles between the crags?'

'Yes,' said Glyn, smiling at her shyly, his head turned slightly away. 'But I don't know that anyone's actually ever heard it.'

'Like something out of Wuthering Heights. Now, your mother is Nesta Gwylym, as was, isn't she? Her people were up from my way, I seem to remember, or my way as was. I never really knew her, but I knew of her. Good, hard-working family. Is she keeping well?'

'Oh, yes thanks,' said Glyn, unaware that she came from the same neck of the woods. 'She knows of you, too.'

'I'll bet,' said Nia, with a small, wry smile, and quickly changed the subject. So there was something between them. But Nia was giving no clues either.

'Do you like pictures?' she enquired of Glyn.

'Well the nearest cinema is quite a way away in Aberystwyth so we don't get to go a lot.'

'No, no, paintings darling. My Art,' she said, nodding at the back wall which was covered in paintings, most of them abstract.

'I don't really know much about art.'

'But is it Art?' put in Luke, lolling all over the sofas and staring up at the ceiling.

'I always say if you have to ask then the answer is no. But then it depends who's asking it,' said Nia, throwing a rather withering glance at her son. 'Luke knows nothing about it either, but worse, he has no interest. I'll teach you.'

The conversation drifted on and, as more drinks were served, became both more animated and meandering. After an hour or so Stockton excused himself, saying he had some papers to look over.

'Hope we'll be seeing a lot more of you round here,' he said, pumping Glyn's hand with his two. He didn't look as if he cared whether they'd ever set eyes on him again. Not long after, Briddy got up too.

'Excuse me, but I'd better start some packing before I'm too pickled.' she said in a quiet, apologetic announcement, and turning to Glyn she said, 'I'm going back to London tomorrow, but I'll see you another time no doubt.'

'Bye bye,' said Glyn. 'Very nice to meet you.'

He hated how formal he sounded. He couldn't help feeling that he was very much out of his depth here, that he sounded unnatural, not knowing the script. He watched Briddy slink out of the room and thought she looked one of the saddest people he had ever met.

'Don't mind Briddy,' said Nia, watching him watching her. 'She has a lot to put up with, but she's not as miserable as she looks. Are you hungry, Glyn? We're usually fairly casual about food here, and we had a late lunch. Come on down to the kitchen and we'll raid the larder.....'

She got up without giving Glyn a chance to explain that he was by now much too drunk to feel hungry and carried on talking, expecting the other two to follow her.

'....and there's something more cosy about sitting round the kitchen table, don't you think? Not so far to reach for the bottles.' She gave one of her tinkling, breezy laughs.

By this time Glyn was indeed feeling distinctly light of head and limb. He was not used to Martinis of any sort, let alone those with the ferocity of Nia's.

He just about made it to the table and slumped down in one of the grandfather chairs. Nia made for the bottles and shaker in the pantry, cooing 'Come to Mama,' brought them over and plonked them in the middle. She seemed to have lost what little restraint she had now that Stockton was no longer on the scene.

'How about some highballs? Now where are the highball glasses?'

Glyn would learn that, as easy going as Nia was, she could be very punctilious about certain things. One of them was having the correct glasses for drinks at all times, for drinks Glyn had never heard of. Her devotion to this was almost sacramental.

'Actually, I'd better be making my way soon,' said Glyn, thinking of the climb home. 'Could I have some coffee?'

'Oh, you'll have to make that yourself,' said Nia. 'Never was much good at it.'

'Where is it?' he asked, looking around the many tall white cupboards lining the walls.

'In the fridge,' said Luke, nodding at the wardrobe-size American appliance.

'In the fridge?' Glyn sounded bemused.

'Well, yes. Don't you keep yours in the fridge at home?'

'Uh, we haven't had a fridge for long and, well, we don't keep much in it.' Certainly not coffee, he thought to himself. These people were strange indeed.

'No fridge? Where'd you keep the milk?'

'In the cow,' said Glyn patiently, as if explaining something obvious to a small child. Nia and Luke gave the kind of laugh that means you don't know whether it's a joke or not. It wasn't.

The coffee turned out to be a bag of beans, which Glyn had never before encountered. He looked from it to Luke.

'Here, I can run to making a cup of coffee,' said Luke. He set about grinding the beans and putting them in a cafetiere, a cigarette drooping from the corner of his mouth.

Nia had lost some of her sparkle, as if the mere act of coffee-making had put the dampers on a good session. Luke though was matching her almost drink for drink and seemed relatively unscathed. Revitalised a little by Luke's strong black brew, Glyn made his departure. Nia had manners enough to thank him for coming, and urge him warmly to come again soon.

'I mean it,' she said. 'It was a real pleasure to meet you.'

Whatever else she was, reflected Glyn, she was great at making you feel appreciated. Luke saw him to the back door.

'Sure you're OK? Could pop you up if you like?'

'Don't be daft. Thanks. I enjoyed meeting your Mum.'

'Oh, think nothing of it. She really enjoyed meeting you too, I could tell.'

He seemed genuinely pleased, and added more to himself, 'She behaved quite well tonight. My turn to come to yours next.' His voice rose to a shout as Glyn set off. 'I'll bring Ma.'

And Glyn swung off up the path, moonlight dancing through the trees, the alarm now helping the caffeine to straighten his gait: alarm at the prospect of two worlds colliding.

When he got home everybody was in bed, and he climbed up the stairs to his bedroom. He didn't switch on the light but went and leant out of his window for a while, looking out at the view. It fairly hummed with stillness, and the whole valley was clear, even the dark woods down to the right which led to Glanharan. He didn't know how he was going to get Luke, let alone Nia, invited up to Bryngwanwyn, but he knew he'd have to find a way.

His mother was sitting in the dark in the armchair by the range. She was watching an old film on the television, divested of its usual tartan blanket covering. TV was not an ever-present entertainment in the farmhouse – watched rather sparingly, in fact. Glyn knew his mother valued these rare moments to herself. His father must be in bed, Tom still out, probably. He couldn't help sitting down and watching it himself, to see if by any chance it was one of Nia's. It wasn't, but it seemed strange, thrilling even, to think it might have been, or that she probably knew some of the people on the screen, as it was from the same era as her heyday.

As if reading his thoughts, his mother said rather wearily, 'And how was your brush with Hollywood?'

He sensed that she was in fact curious to hear something of the evening, despite her show of indifference.

'It was good. They're quite nice people when you get to know them a bit.'

'You're honoured, I'm sure.'

'In fact, they were asking when they could meet you,' Glyn said as casually as he could, looking anywhere but at his mother. He had no idea how she would react. There was a pause, as the silver figures on the screen flashed a blue light round the room.

'Suppose they've invited you down. Perhaps you'd better ask her and that boy of hers up here for tea one Saturday afternoon. Only common courtesy. And let no-one say we can't show that.'

He was surprised at how little resistance she put up when it came to it.

'What, that we're courteous – or common?'

The joke fell flat, and his mother gave him one of her looks.

'How about a week on Saturday?' asked Glyn, pressing his advantage

'If she's got a spare hour or two in her diary,' said his mother, with no discernible sign of irony.

5

Glyn grew more and more nervous as Saturday morning turned into afternoon. He kept a watchful eye on the lane as he went about his jobs, trying not to show that he was on tenterhooks. The visit was fraught with pitfalls, which kept going round in his head. He was dimly aware that Nia was one of those women whom other women don't like very much, but he couldn't say why.

After dinner Nain did the ironing, as she always did, on a couple of thick old blankets folded over on the kitchen table. He'd never thought anything about this before but now he found he was anxious that blankets were put away out of sight before the guests arrived. It embarrassed him somehow that they didn't have an ironing board like anyone else. At the same time he found his own embarrassment embarrassing. Why couldn't he be pleased that his family had their own customs and characteristics, different from the herd?

He was looking through the kitchen window, but pretending not to. They'd have to come in through the kitchen - the front door was stuck shut and it was never used. New visitors had to be headed off before they started down the front path towards it, and shepherded round the back of the house. At last, at about five o'clock, he caught sight of the Rover turning in by the milk stand, its chrome flashing in the sun.

'Mam, they're coming,' he shouted.

She'd been busy in the front room laying out the tea. Despite her mysterious antipathy towards the Glanharan people, she had put a lot of effort into providing the best: boiling a ham, carefully arranging a huge mixed salad with a pretty pattern of tomato, cucumber and egg on top, baking cakes and tarts. She came out into the kitchen and wiped her hands on her pinny. Oh God, surely she was going to take that off? Just when he thought she'd forgotten and that he'd have to say something, she whisked it off and stuffed it in the drawer of the huge oak kitchen cabinet, and Glyn felt sheepish. Then he saw the goose wing Nain used for dusting was on the cabinet shelf. He pounced on it and put it back in the pantry without his mother seeing, ashamed of being ashamed of it. It was as if he were seeing everything through different, critical, more cultured eyes.

He and his mother went out into the back yard as the Rover pulled up. Nain was fussing over the best tea service and his father was reading his newspaper by the range.

'Hello,' said Nia, stepping out of the car regally and holding out her hand to his mother. 'Glyn's told us so much about you and I've so been looking forward to this. Thank you for the invitation.' She handed over a huge bouquet of flowers. 'This is my son, Luke.'

Even his mother thawed slightly under this effusive charm offensive, but was flustered by the unaccustomed flowers.

'Come on in,' she said, and introduced them to her mother and husband. Glyn could see straight away that his father was taken with this glamorous creature, and could see that his mother could see it. Nain gave her a good look up and down without troubling to conceal it. 'Very pleased to meet you,' she said. She looked anything but.

His mother busied herself reaching for a cut glass vase from the top shelf of the cabinet.

'Now, how about a nice cup of tea?'

'Never touch the stuff,' said Nia sweetly. There was a general freezing of action at this announcement. Nain was bent over the kitchen table arranging the cups but the clinking stopped as she gave a sidelong glance to Nia and then to her daughter.

'How about something stronger?' suggested Glyn's father cheerily. 'I don't usually drink in the house myself,' he added, catching his wife's frown.

'Well, that makes one of us,' said Nia, breaking into her arpeggio of a laugh. 'Gin and tonic? Just a large one, then. Not too much tonic.'

'Same for me,' piped up Luke.

In fact there was not much hard drink kept in the house, but gin was one thing they did have, largely to revive ailing lambs when they were brought into the warmth of the kitchen during the winter lambing season.

'I'm afraid we don't have any ice,' said Glyn, abashed by their lack of cocktail ingredients. 'Or lemon.'

'Oh well, all the more room for the gin,' said Nia.

His father went into the pantry to get a couple of bottles of beer for him and Glyn.

'We've got plenty of gin,' he said and Glyn dreaded further explanation. 'Keep it for the lambs.'

'Yes, we used to do that,' said Nia unexpectedly. 'Capful of gin, then into a cardboard box in the bottom oven.'

This served to ease the atmosphere slightly, the realisation that this creature was not so alien after all. Even Nain raised her eyebrows and gave a slight nod of approval. They proceeded into the front room for the strange tea, with Nain shuffling in and out tending to them like some old family retainer, giving odd winks in Nia's direction. Glyn and his family sipped their tea while Nia and Luke slugged back their gin.

Conversation was a little stiff at first as nobody seemed to want to ask Nia about her early life in Wales or the Hollywood years and she didn't seem to want to volunteer any information. She soon got into her stride though, talking about her life in Hollywood, the stars she knew, and then later her work in television in New York, her beautiful home in Sag Harbour on Long Island, her flat in Manhattan. His father mentioned some of her first, fairly successful films just after the war.

'We loved you in *A Midnight Clear*,' he said, beaming. It was probably the film Nia was best known for, run with regularity on television at Christmas. Even his mother agreed. It was the first time Glyn had ever heard of either of his parents going to the pictures.

'I hated that film, it was lousy. Made me out to be little more than a tart, fawning over men for trinkets.'

Nain was clearing away the teacups and on hearing the word tart, knocked one over on the tray with a clatter.

'So you believe in all this sex equality then do you?' asked Glyn's father.

'Equality? Who wants to be equal with men? We've got to set our sights far higher than that, haven't we, Mrs Bennett?' and she gave Glyn's mother a gentle elbow in the ribs. She looked shocked at Nia's nerve, but then suddenly gave a faint gasp of a laugh. Glyn noticed Nain giving his mother a rather pointed look.

'We're not used to having such glamorous guests,' said Glyn's father.

'Oh, well, glamour is best viewed from afar,' said Nia, 'or with unjaded eyes. After a while you start to see all the cardboard under the tinsel. A bit like Christmas presents - they're much nicer all wrapped up and waiting to be opened. It's always a slight disappointment when you do.'

'Is that why you came back?' asked Glyn's mother, 'because you got tired of the glamorous life?'

'Oh, it's always a lot of little things, rather than one big thing. But I did begin to get bored with it all. And the stage can be a lonely place when you don't want to be there. I know it seemed I was lucky to have all I did, and I was, but the tragedy was I stopped feeling it.'

She told then about the time she was flying down to Cuba for location shooting on her last feature film *Havana Hideaway*, 'in the old days before Castro'. They were passing over the Florida Keys, where the sea shimmered 'like emerald satin' and was so clear you could see right through to the ocean floor. The sand in the beach was almost white, and you could see the bathers in the surf. They were on a narrow shelf by the shore where the water was relatively shallow, but suddenly the seabed fell away dramatically in a seemingly bottomless abyss. His parents listened to this as if they were children being told a story. Even Nain had stood stock still, teapot in hand, as if she'd been transported to far-off places. This was the magic that Nia Barry could weave.

'It made me think how vulnerable we all are to the tides of fortune, no matter how happy or secure we think we are, or others think we are, it could all disappear in a second.'

By this time Nia had proffered her glass for refills more than once. She had hardly touched her food, and refused all offer of cake or tart. This had not gone unnoticed by the other women. All that work gone to waste, although Luke had tucked in as if he had not eaten all day. Glyn was worried that in this rather maudlin mood Nia might reveal more than she or his parents would wish.

'I've got to go out to feed the lambs,' he said. 'Want to come with me?' He was surprised when Nia and Luke took up his offer.

He led them outside with a wave of relief. Nia was slightly unsteady on her feet as they made their way to the old wooden barn, not helped by her high heels and the slippery cobbles in the farm yard. Luke kept a guiding hand under her elbow. Inside, in a little clearing in the hay bales, a dozen or so lambs frolicked to greet them. Glyn got a large bucket with as many teats sticking out round the bottom. They went to get some milk from the cowshed where his brothers were washing the cows' udders ready for milking machines. They gave his friends curt, shy nods and went about their work.

'Oh look,' said Nia. 'They've got their names chalked up on the beams above their stalls. How cute. Daisy II, Buttercup... It's like something out of a storybook.'

Alun and Glyn exchanged bemused looks.

'Didn't you have names for your milkers when you were a girl?' asked Glyn.

The smile vanished from Nia's face. 'No, just sheep and fat cattle.'

'You seem to have names for everything,' put in Luke. 'Cows, fields.... Why on earth would anyone want to name a field?'

'So you know where you're going,' said Alun, shooting Glyn another puzzled smile.

Alun filled Glyn's bucket with the first milk and they went back into the old barn to feed the lambs. Nia seemed genuinely charmed with the whole proceedings. Luke could not have looked more bored. Glyn noticed that he'd been uncharacteristically silent throughout the visit. Nia had a turn at holding the bucket while the lambs fed – they could be quite rough and the bucket needed a bit of holding – but Luke declined the invitation with a shake of his head. As they left the barn Nia noticed the sheepdog Cymro lying on its chain. He could be unpredictable, sometimes barking a lot at strangers and sometimes taking no notice.

'Ah, come here boy, come here.' The dog blinked and yawned.

'He only responds to Welsh,' said Glyn.

'Tyd yma, Tyd yma,' said Nia and the dog leapt up and strained at his tether, jumping up at Nia. It was extremely odd to hear Nia speak Welsh to the dog. She bent down to stroke him and fell over in the mud.

'I'd better be getting Ma back,' Luke said quietly, much to Glyn's relief, as they went back up to the house. 'Time to hitch up the wagons, Ma,' he said more loudly to his mother, trailing slightly behind. Glyn noticed they often talked to each other in quotes from films.

'And we'll go down to the Mucky Duck for a few,' he said to Glyn.

Glyn called inside the house that the guests were leaving. His parents came out and his father gave Nia a peck on the cheek. It was very unlike him. He'd clearly enjoyed himself. His mother said a cordial goodbye as they piled into the Rover, her arms folded.

'I've enjoyed it all so much,' said Nia through the open window of the car, a little sobered now by the fresh air. 'You have such a lovely home and family,' she said to his mother, and it seemed genuine admiration. 'It takes me back.'

His mother responded with a brief nod and smile. Glyn now saw that he'd been a fool to worry so much, to feel so awkward about his family's quirks. Nia seemed as enchanted by his world as he was by hers.

'You must all come down to Glanharan one of these days,' said Nia.

His mother nodded again, but something about her manner suggested that wasn't going to happen.

'I'm just popping down to the pub with Luke,' said Glyn to his mother.

'Ah, alright,' she said, crumpling her mouth.

They dropped Nia off at Glanharan. She waved them a cheery goodbye and lurched into the house.

'Will she be alright?' asked Glyn as Luke sped towards the pub.

'Of course,' said Luke. 'She's just warming up. Briddy's down from London and Stockton's back from New York. She's got her little helpers around her.'

By now the Mucky Duck crowd had got more used to Luke; indeed most of them enjoyed his cocky ways and exotic tales. Johnny Jones was at his usual place in the bar but deigned to join them at the table by the window. It had become their usual table. For all his fancy ways, Luke seemed to like a certain order, a certain routine.

He asked Johnny Jones about Llanfair and whether there were any more dances coming up.

'No, it's only an annual bash' said Johnny Jones.

But Luke persisted.

'I presume it has a local?' he enquired. 'Nice place. Nice girls. How about an expedition up there one night?'

He gently pushed Johnny Jones into agreeing to a night out there the next Saturday. Glyn said he had to go to his Nain's eightieth birthday party at the hotel in Aberharan. He was somewhat taken aback by Luke's eagerness for an expedition to Llanfair. He wondered what was behind it. Maybe he was tiring of this pub with the same old people saying the same old things week in, week out. In a way, Glyn couldn't blame him. He looked around, trying to see things through his new friend's eyes. It couldn't in any way be described as an exciting place. And that's what Luke seemed to crave - excitement. Danger, even. Yet Glyn couldn't help feeling a sense of betrayal.

'Well, we'll just have to struggle on without you,' said Luke.

When Luke was at the gents, Glyn took the opportunity to broach something with Johnny Jones that had been on his mind, but it wasn't easy.

'Look,' he said, 'I'm sorry if I've been spending quite a bit of time with him lately.'

'No need to explain, boy,' said Johnny Jones.

'It's just that he sort of draws you in, involves you in things before you've had time to think.'

'Oh aye, I know what you mean.'

'I don't think he's got any real friends,' said Glyn, and hoped Johnny Jones would understand the unspoken words 'like us.'

'Oh well, we'll just have to do, won't we?'

Glyn was glad that they seemed to understand each other.

They'd sunk a few pints when time was called but Luke again insisted he was alright to drive. Indeed he seemed largely unaffected and sped through the lanes in his usual reckless style, flicking the ash from his cigarette just short of the ashtray.

'Coming in for a nightcap?' he said, hopping out and slamming the door, giving Glyn no chance to decline.

Nia, Briddy and Stockton were in the living room. Nia was well in her cups, lolling on the sofa with her head and right arm thrown over the back of it. Ella Fitzgerald was on the record player singing '*I'll take Manhattan*'.

'Greetings,' she slurred, stirring slightly. 'Come and get this party back on its feet.'

Stockton swirled the ice in the bottom of his empty glass and shot them a look of annoyance, whether at Nia's drunkenness or their arrival it was hard to tell.

'Don't you think you've had enough?' he asked presently as she reached wildly for a bottle on the drinks trolley.

'I know when I've had enough,' said Nia belligerently. 'I've still got too much blood in my alcohol system.'

She edged up the sofa jerkily towards Stockton and started slapping him gently and playfully on his cheeks, but then the slaps got harder, too hard.

'When you're slapped you'll take it and like it",' she said, whistling through a tight top lip like Bogart. Stockton swiped her hand away. She reached up again and squeezed his lips into a pout.

'I'm saaaarry,' she said in a rasping American accent, moving Stockton's lips to the words.

'Glyn, did I ever tell you about the time I met my dear husband? It was in a hotel in New York and we were in a lift. We couldn't even wait to get a room...'

Briddy got up from her chair and set her sherry glass down on a side table.

'Nia, it's time for bed,' she said in a businesslike manner. 'Come on Luke, give me a hand".

Nia threw her arm in the air as the pair manhandled her towards the door.

'My regiment leaves at dawn,' they could catch her shouting as they manoeuvred her out of the room.

Stockton studied Glyn, his eyes narrowed in the indecision of whether or not to speak.

'You're probably wondering why I sit back and allow my wife to drink herself to death?'

'Not really. It's none of my business.'

'It's lots of people's business,' said Stockton sharply. 'Well, it's no good trying to stop her,' he said to his empty glass. 'What do I do? Spend all my time searching out her empty bottles? Tell her to quit or I leave? That's a loser's game. She'd fight me. You've got to make it easy for her. So she can fight with herself.'

Glyn was at a loss for something adequate to say. Stockton had had a few himself. Glyn didn't like him, and he was sure the feeling was mutual.

'You're probably right,' he said inadequately. 'Why does she drink so much?'

'To pass the time,' said Stockton, as if it were only too obvious. 'A drunk is never bored, and she gets bored very easily. You must remember that she is used to being feted and fought over. But in the end, that bored her too.'

Luke came back in jingling the car keys. Some of the sparkle had left him too.

'Come on. I'll run you up,' he said.

Glyn knew he should really refuse. Luke was in no fit state to drive. But Glyn was in no fit state to walk.

'Does your mother often get like that?'

'Oh yes,' said Luke.

'Does it worry you?'

'Nah.'

But Glyn suspected he wasn't being completely honest.

Next afternoon towards teatime Glyn was in the kitchen reading the paper. His mother was boiling bits of pig on the stove. They'd killed the pig and got a local butcher up to cut it up. His mother boiled all the leftover bits - Glyn could see a bit of an ear and a trotter dancing in the scummy bubbles - to make brawn. It was a horrible smell, but when the brawn was cold and sliced it was irresistible. The small-paned kitchen window was all fogged up with the steam and it gave Glyn a sense of being cut off from the outside world. He took advantage of the moment to ask his mother about her impressions of their visitors.

'What I expected, really.'

'What did you expect, then?'

'What she was.'

Glyn kept his patience.

'Well, what was that? Did you like her?'

'Oh, she's alright,' said his mother, beginning to lose hers. 'Although I've never seen a woman drink that much at that time of the day.'

His mother did not approve of women drinking more than a glass or two of something appropriate like sherry, but tolerated it in men as a fact of life.

'Why she wanted to come back here I can't imagine,' she said, clutching a loaf to her chest and sawing pieces off with great gusto. 'She'd made a life for herself. That boy of hers was quite polite, I suppose...... A bit of a charmer. I don't know. I can't see how any good will come of it.'

6

Glyn didn't see Luke for three or four weeks after that. Summer was at its busy, noisy height and there was much work to be done preparing for the hay harvest. It was all hands on deck. On Cae Ifor and Big Cae Ifor, the flatter fields above the house, Glyn and his brothers mowed, turned and tedded the hay ready for baling. There began the usual argument between Alun, who did the baling, and his father about the right way to bale a field of hay. Glyn's father held that it was quicker baling right around the edge of the field and then moving in concentric squares to the middle. Alun preferred to go up and down the field in strips, like mowing a lawn. Glyn's father argued that his method involved less time-consuming turning of the baler. Alun tirelessly pointed out that while this may be true for the outer turns, the more you got into the middle the more you were turning, and right in the middle you had almost to turn on a sixpence. The argument was pointless and anyway Alun always did it his way.

After that there would be the corn harvest. The Bennetts now borrowed a combine from a neighbour. Glyn could still remember the days when the threshing machine used to go round from farm to farm, requiring twelve or so men to bring in the harvest. It was a lumbering, terrifying monster, black with oil. Glyn remembered it being pulled by the old blue Fordson Major tractor up the steep, rutted lane above Bryngwanwyn towards the neighbouring farm. He would watch it inch and lurch its way, thinking it would tip over at any moment. His father could remember it being pulled by horses, which must have been even more perilous.

Once the old machine had been installed by the top barn at Bryngwanwyn, the men would bring in the wheat sheaves by the cartload to be threshed. As its great wheels and belts whirred noisily around Glyn watched fearfully in case anyone got too close, especially one if his family. He was haunted by stories of men who had got their arms caught in the belt and suffered loss of limb or worse.

His mother and Nain would bring baskets of doorstop sandwiches of his Nain's own bread and butter, and stone flagons of cider and beer, called Coopers, after the local wine merchant who supplied them.

At the end of the exhausting day the men, dusty with the chaff that got everywhere, would trundle down to the house for the harvest supper, and Glyn would be swept by a wave of relief that it had all passed off without injury.

In the kitchen two tables were placed end to end and every chair in the house brought out. The men would sit down and the women would serve them a supper of cold meats and new potatoes, pickles and beetroot, all laid out in huge quantities in the biggest dishes they possessed. Wooden crates of beer stood in the pantry. It was Glyn's job to make sure that no-

62

one finished one without a new one being put in front of him. The men spoke a language almost of their own and they discussed how the day had gone, how the wheat had threshed, how much grain it had yielded and how good a quality it was. And, of course, the old days and how much harder but better they were. Each farm, apparently, was known for its fare, its own speciality. Glyn had never been able to find out what Bryngwanwyn's was.

Now there was smaller, more modern and efficient machinery for both harvests, right down to the escalator to lift the bales of hay and straw to the top of the barns. But the work seemed just as hard. In the hay harvest Glyn's job was to stack the bales on the trailer as fast as his brothers could pitchfork them up to him. Each bale had its place on the trailer, so not an inch of space was wasted. At the front end they went lengthwise between the struts which supported the slatted wooden ends. Then in an interlocking pattern like a parquet floor so they would keep their place as the trailer was stacked several bales high until they were jutting out over the tractor at the top of the ends.

Glyn had been too busy in the past month or so to give much thought to his future. He knew somewhere deep down that he wanted to go out into the world and make his way. He just didn't know if he had the courage. His father and brothers liked the idea of him going to university. They knew he was bright and that there was no room for a fourth on the farm now. Not that there didn't always seem enough for him to do. His father had never quite understood why Glyn had to do so much homework for his A levels, and seemed to suspect he was trying to dodge the farm work.

Glyn saw Luke in the Mucky Duck one Saturday, and learnt that Luke too had been busy. On the trip to Llanfair with Johnny Jones he'd met

Emma Peel in the local pub and she'd thawed slightly and given him her phone number, which Luke lost no time in putting to good use. He'd gone out with her a couple of times and they were getting to like each other. Her name was Sian. Luke wanted Glyn to meet her. Glyn didn't want to commit to anything as it was awkward when they were in the middle of the hay harvest. His father and brothers usually liked them all to go for a drink on Friday and Saturday nights during the harvest, when the beer went down exceptionally well, the first two or three pints barely touching the sides. Sometimes they would all go to his father's local, another pub in Aberharan. But other times, if they were coming to the end of a field, or if the sky clouded over threatening rain, they would plough on through dusk to get it all in, going down to the farmhouse afterwards for a few bottles of beer.

Glyn had half-promised to go out with them the following Saturday. The forecast was good and they thought they'd have one field cleared by late afternoon. As it turned out it took them a bit longer and by seven o'clock his father and Tom still had two or three stooks in the top corner of the field to load. Glyn was on top of the trailer, kneeing the bales into place, and as he turned to pick up the next from the loaded pikel, as they called their pitchforks, he saw two tall figures climbing over the stile at the bottom of the field and making their way up towards the workers.

'Must be friends of thine,' Alun shouted up to Glyn.

'Well ah, it's thee friend from Glanharan,' said his father, sticking his pikel into the stubble and leaning on it, ready for a rest. His father and brothers still used the old, familiar form of address between each other, especially in a traditional work setting like this. It was more or less kept for the family though - outside they tried to speak what they thought of as more correct English.

'Bist 'ee thinking of getting an early off?' asked his father.

'Nah,' said Glyn. 'We've only got a few more to do.' He steadied himself on the hayload, which swayed slightly every time he moved. He stood with his legs apart and arms on his hips, watching the couple walk up the field. It didn't feel quite right to see Luke on the hayfield. Alun sat on a bale and took a swig from the flagon of beer, himself ready for a bit of a breather.

'Hullo there,' said Luke very loudly, as if shouting to someone in the next field, and waving wildly as if at someone out at sea.

' 'Lo,' said the three, not quite in unison.

'Have yo' come to lend a hand?' asked his father. 'Yo' look as if yo'd be a bit of use if yo' put your back into it,' he said to Luke.

'Oh, you look as if you're managing alright,' said Luke with an easy grin. 'This is Sian.'

The group made the halting, sparse small-talk of interrupted work, welcome as it was. It was something different to see a young, good-looking woman in the hayfield. When they found out Sian was from Llanfair they made the usual local jokes, the way the people of one area would try to outdo a neighbouring one. Llanfair people were deemed over-careful with their money. Sian gave as good as she got, used to such gambits.

'Well, is this all you've left to do?' said Luke. 'Doesn't look as if you'll be long. Then we'll take you for a well-deserved libation.' He winked up at Glyn.

'Aye, we'll just finish this off and you can have a lift back down to the house,' said his father.

'What in?' asked Luke, looking round.

'On the top of the load of course,' said Alun.

When they were done, Alun grabbed Sian by the waist and hoisted her level with the floor of the trailer, so she could get a toe-hold to climb up top. She took it in her stride, reaching for Glyn's outstretched hand and finding holes where the corner of the bales met. Luke was left to his own devices, and had to have a couple of goes before he got the hang of it. The others watched, enjoying the entertainment. When the three of them were atop Glyn told them to lie flat and grab hold of the strings of two bales.

'"Fasten your seat belts. it's going to be a bumpy ride",' said Luke.

Glyn's father jumped on the back of the tractor and Alun started it up with a roar and a plume of black smoke spurting from the chimney.

'You'll have to hold on tight,' Glyn told them. 'It swings about a bit.'

By now the day was dimming into the slate blue of dusk. Stretched out on the hay, their eyes met the hazy waves of hills on the other side of the valley, ebbing away in ever-lightening shades of bluish-grey.

The trailer moved fairly smoothly down the flattened field, but began rocking alarmingly as it moved on to the deep rough tracks of the lane going down to the house. It always seemed touch and go at times, whether the hay cart would topple over. Glyn could not remember that it ever had, or his father ever talking about such an accident.

They had another half an hour unloading the bales into the barn. Luke and Sian sat on the gate watching them, Luke with a stalk of hay between his teeth. When they came to the last bale, Alun said, as he always did, 'That's the one we've been looking for.'

Luke jumped off the gate and reached up to help Sian down, but she brushed him aside and jumped down too.

'Bet you're ready for a pint now,' said Luke to Glyn.

'Better have a bath first,' said Glyn. 'Full of hay dust.'

He motioned to Luke and Sian to follow him into the kitchen. Glyn's mother was getting supper ready and looked slightly annoyed at the intrusion but wiped her hands on her apron and shook hands with Sian with her usual cordiality and said a How D'you Do to Luke.

'We're just off into town for a drink,' said Glyn.

'You'll need something inside you first,' said his mother. 'Will you have something to eat with us?' she asked of the other two.

They said they'd already eaten and Glyn said he'd had enough sandwiches during the day and would have something later.

'Oh, OK,' she said with a resigned shrug. She liked to feed people.

It wasn't long before Glyn was ready and the three of them went out to the Rover, parked at an odd angle in front of the backyard wall. They made it to the Aberharan Hotel by about nine. Sian proved to be good company, never stuck for something to say, making gentle fun of Luke and his ways and answering him with clever, witty remarks. She taught English and French at Llanfair High School and Glyn found an instant rapport with her, discussing books and writers. Luke looked a little put out, although he was quite widely read and joined in with flippant, dismissive comments. He said Sian was coming to lunch the next day to meet his mother. Sian looked at Glyn and made wide eyes and a forced smile. Luke invited Glyn to come along. It would mean missing Sunday dinner at home, but his mother was slowly getting more resigned to Glyn's gallivanting, as she called it.

Arriving at Glanharan at half twelve the next day, he found Nia in an excited mood.

'Luke's gone to pick up his new paramour,' she said to Glyn, pouring him a glass of sherry. 'I can't wait to meet her. We're doing everything properly and having a real Sunday lunch with roast lamb and all the trimings. Well, Briddy's doing everything properly, I should say. I can't cook to save my life. It's as much as I can do to open things.'

Nia's attitude to food was somewhat hit or miss, and when she decided to push the boat out she did it in style, or rather got someone else like Briddy to do the heavy lifting. Glyn sometimes wondered how she and Luke managed when Briddy wasn't there. He expected she bought things ready-made, which was something of a cardinal sin at the farm, especially shop-bought cake. His Nain still made the family's bread and he could remember when she churned the butter too, in a wooden barrel in the barn which swivelled round and round as you turned a large black handle. It was one of Glyn's chores when he was little - hard, boring work. He remembered the first time he tasted sliced bread in the Milk Bar, which he thought heavenly and far preferred to Nain's home-made. He used to call it Milk Bar bread, and once asked his mother if they could have it at home. He got a clip around the ear. Now, though, Nain no longer had the strength to churn butter, and no-one else had the time or the will. Margarine was now on the weekly shopping list of things the farm couldn't produce itself.

Nia quizzed Glyn about what Sian was like, which Glyn thought a little pointless seeing as she'd be meeting her for herself in a few moments, and gave polite but evasive answers, feeling for some reason a little shy of describing Sian.

'Oh don't be so diffident, Glyn,' and then clearly saw the puzzled look on his face. 'Look it up.'

Glyn was just grasping for something to say, when they heard the roar of the Rover and the squeal of breaks and crunch of gravel as it pulled up outside the front door. Nia and Glyn went out into the porch to greet them. Luke bounded up the steps and Sian followed behind him with her natural amble and smile. He beamed as Nia held out her hand and welcomed Sian. She seemed charmed and intrigued by her, and her eyes kept darting back in Sian's direction. Glyn guessed that she was very different from the girls Luke usually brought home. Nia put her arm around her and guided her into the living room where a vast glass platter of canapes and the sherry decanter and glasses were arranged on the coffee table.

After a glass or two they went through double, sliding doors into the oak-panelled dining room. The table was covered in white linen, silver and crystal, a huge bunch of red roses in a glass bowl in the centre. Lunch was a very pleasant affair, and Nia couldn't have been more charming to Sian. Briddy had indeed done everything properly: but a lot of the food was new to Glyn. There was prawn avocado to start, served in large wine glasses. Glyn had read the word avocado in books, but didn't know what it was. He had somehow associated it with lawyers. He glanced surreptitiously over at Sian to check that he was eating it properly, and using the right cutlery and glass. It was as if she vaguely realised this, and picked up the outside fork slowly and deliberately, and proffered her glass before him.

The lamb was served with asparagus - another novelty. He liked that too. And on the sideboard was a huge meringue affair with cream, strawberries and a fruit Glyn couldn't identify - thin round green slices with black seeds in the middle. Next to it was something he did recognise - half a Stilton with black grapes and walnuts. There was St Emillion and Pouilly-Fume to drink. Once he'd got over his nervousness at dealing with the unfamiliar, he started to enjoy his gastronomic adventure.

'Do you think the wine goes well with the lamb, Glyn?' asked Nia.

Glyn was unused to wine and wouldn't have a clue how to answer. He glanced at Nia to see if it was some kind of test. But she was merely pushing her meagre portions around the plate, hardly touching a thing, and didn't seem particularly interested in his reply. She was just making conversation.

He side-stepped the question. 'The lamb's lovely.'

'Bill Butch,' said Nia unexpectedly, using the local term for the butcher in Llanfair.

'The St Emilion's excellent,' said Sian, as back-up. Her eyebrows were raised in surprise, as if she too were taken aback at the Bill Butch reference.

Nia fired questions unashamedly at Sian, who answered with grace and humour. Her father had also been a teacher and was now retired. She'd got a degree at Bristol University, and had travelled quite widely in Europe. She had been married for a brief time. About three years. She had got married too young, picked the wrong man. No, it was not amicable. He ran off with someone else. No, there were no children. No, she never saw him. No, she did not know where he was and did not care.

Glyn glanced at Nia furtively, trying to gauge her reaction to the fact that her young son was going out with an older divorcee. She seemed fascinated by everything Sian said, leaning with her elbows on the table studying her carefully.

When they'd finished, everyone congratulated Nia on the excellent lunch. She waved all compliments towards Briddy who beamed in pleasure. She'd barely said a word throughout the meal.

Nia got up and summoned Sian for a tour of the house, playing the role of chatelaine to a tee. Luke and Glyn trooped behind.

'We haven't finished everything yet,' she said. 'There are still a couple of bedrooms to do, and we haven't even looked at the attics.'

After the kitchen Nia showed them into Stockton's study, lined on two sides with floor-to-ceiling bookshelves, and on the other two with a leaf green paper and prints of hunting scenes. There was an oak, roll-top desk, a green-shaded banker's lamp and a swivel leather chair. To Glyn's eyes, it looked very American.

Then there was another sitting room with a Steinway grand piano and a harp. Nia called it the Music Room.

'I know it's a little pretentious,' said Nia. 'But there you are.'

Luke nudged Sian in the ribs and winked back at Glyn.

Up the polished oak stairs, with the spindles painted white, the first room they came to was the master bedroom with an en suite bathroom completely tiled in white.

'That's lovely bed linen,' said Sian, as if she felt she had to show some reaction to this tour. They looked at the blue and white striped pattern, which reminded Glyn of the ticking on the mattresses at home.

'Brushed cotton,' said Nia. 'I always insist on it.'

Luke's bedroom was a complete mess with clothes flung everywhere: dirty ashtrays, mugs and wine glasses dotted here and there, books tossed about half-read, records everywhere. Nia, so fastidious in certain things, seemed to accept this was entirely a natural state for her son's bedroom to be in, and uttered no word of apology. They passed Briddy's room ('We won't go in there. God knows what - or who - she's got secreted away'), but looked in at one of the guest rooms, decorated all in yellow.

'It's as much as we can do to stop ourselves calling it The Yellow Room", said Nia.

'You do call it The Yellow Room, Ma,' said Luke, trailing behind them making a great show of his boredom.

On one side of the house was a third floor of rooms, clearly for servants, which had not been touched. A yellowish plaster crumbled off the walls here and there to reveal the lath underneath. From there, there was a winding back staircase which came out opposite the kitchen door.

Throughout all this Sian had smiled and nodded politely as Nia told her she had bought this fabric at Bloomingdales or that picture at Sotheby's. Glyn found himself absorbed with the transformation of the old ruin. It was all done in such style. He'd never seen anything like it, although there was something very faintly familiar. He finally worked out that it reminded him of all those forties black and white films. It was a Hollywood version of a great house – a film set. Style without character, Glyn couldn't help thinking. Finally Luke could take no more and suggested a walk down to the river.

'We can take some nets and see what we can catch,' he said. 'I spotted some in one of those junk rooms.'

'You three go right ahead,' said Nia. 'I've done enough walking. I always say that too much exercise is dangerous,' she said in an aside to Sian. 'I'm going to have a rest, and Briddy here has got the clearing up to do.'

As the three walked down the drive, Sian questioned Luke about Briddy.

'Is she some kind of servant?'

'No, she's Ma's best friend really. Has been for years. She came over from Barbados with the WAAFs during the war and stayed on as a nurse.'

'I'd have loved to talk to her, but couldn't get a word in edgeways. She seemed really nice.'

Luke seemed to grasp that Sian disapproved of the way his mother treated her friend, and that further explanation was required.

'Briddy likes cooking and doing all the things for Ma,' he said. 'She's a bit lonely really.'

'No man in her life?'

'She's got a lover called Henry in London who won't leave his wife and she can't see him at weekends, or very much at all really. But she's besotted by him so can't do anything. She's very intelligent and all that - now she's got a job in a big firm in the City, near where Henry works. She sometimes complains that he only wants her for her brain.'

Glyn saw Luke shoot a sideways glance at Sian to see if she had got the answer to her questions.

'She was a bit nervous about coming here at first, you know, being the only black person and all. But Ma told her it would be alright.'

'But your mother does treat her a little like a personal slave,' said Sian quietly, chewing on a blade of grass.

'Well, you know Ma. She treats everyone like her personal slave. Me included. But they think the world of each other. Ma says they complete a circle. Whatever that means. I guess they both get something out of it.'

Luke thought for a moment as they ambled along, and squinted up at the sun.

'Do you think Ma's right - will it be alright? For Briddy, I mean.'

Sian smiled. 'Oh, most of us aren't that bad. We reserve most of our prejudice for people from the next town or valley. Or the English.' She elbowed Glyn in the ribs.

'Yeah, I've noticed,' said Luke.

They got to the river where it was shallow and stony just below the bridge. Glyn duly set to untangling the nets and rods and made to start fishing, but looked back at Luke and Sian who were laying a tartan rug out on the bank and obviously had no intention of doing anything other than lying there. He felt like they did - just wanted to lie back on the grass and have more wine and soak up the sun.

He went to join them, but felt awkward about lying on the rug with them as they lolled so easily, so he lay with one leg on and one leg off. He looked up at the perfect blue sky, listened to the perfect summer silence, broken only by the trickle of the water and the faraway drone of a biplane which was a familiar feature of Sunday afternoons.

His thoughts drifted back to the day he came down with his niece and nephew. Was it really just a few weeks ago? For a fleeting moment he could feel that carefree joy that he envied in them. It was almost like a caress, like a cool gust of air on a hot day. But as soon as he started thinking about it, it evaporated, like the memory of a dream which is gone as soon as it's remembered. It was what he thought of as 'a moment': he had had them since he was a young child. It was an almost indefinable sensation of something known but forgotten, which contained something akin to deja vu, but more - a hint of something unknowable.

These moments came unbidden and unbiddable, brought on perhaps by a certain trick of the light in a certain place, smoke wafting from a cottage in the woods, ivy creeping over the crumbling bricks of an old ruin. It was like a glimpse of something eternal, comforting, yet challenging, like being in a cosy doze but knowing that something is about to niggle you awake.

He looked across at Luke and Sian and envied their ease. He thought how wonderful were the faint smile wrinkles at the corners of Sian's eyes. He didn't want the afternoon to end. And suddenly he had the first tiny inkling that this couldn't last, this new world he'd been drawn into, that something was about to go horribly wrong.

7

Luke's next project was for a weekend in London, to show Glyn 'some of the usual haunts.' Glyn had been there only once, several years before on a school day trip, so he was sorely tempted. But when the invitation came by telephone, some of Glyn's original wariness about getting too chummy with Luke resurfaced automatically. He explained that it was a busy time on the farm, with the harvest coming up.

'Thought you'd finished the harvest,' said Luke.

'That was hay. Corn next.'

'Good Lord. Then now's the time to go, before it kicks off for real,' said Luke, not unreasonably, Glyn had to admit to himself.

'And anyway, if you've got to make a decision about leaving the nest and venturing out into the big wide world, you may as well see something of it.'

'Is Sian coming?'

'Can't. Some family thing on,' said Luke, as if this were the most tedious thing in the world.

Glyn found himself being talked into it and saying 'Alright then,' although he knew it probably wouldn't go down too well with his family, particularly his mother. He'd also have to get more adept at standing up to Luke, he decided. He could twist him round his little finger and always seemed to be the one in control. But the trip would at least give him the chance to get to know his friend a little better. Luke remained something of an enigma. Glyn still didn't know much about his interests, apart from women.

Luke took charge of the agenda.

'We can stay in Stockton's flat in Soho. He's in New York for a while. We won't take the old jalopy, it'll take too long. Is there a train?'

'We'd have to drive to Machynlleth and take the Cambrian Express from there.' Glyn still felt the need to use the conditional.

'The Cambrian Express, no less. How many days does that take?'

'Five hours or so.'

'Perhaps Ma will give us a lift to the station.'

They settled on the weekend after next. Within his mother's hearing he asked his father if he could have the weekend off.

'Oh, ah, expect we'll just about manage without thee for a day or two,' said his father straightaway.

'What do you want to go to London for?' asked his mother.

'Oh, come on Mam. There's loads to do in London. I don't get away all that often,' said Glyn.

'And where are you going to be staying?' she said.

'In Stockton's flat. That's Nia's husband.'

'Where's that?'

'In.....,' and there was a tiny but telling pause, '....Soho.'

His father gave a wolf whistle and his mother both of them a scowl.

'Well, it's a chance for the boy to see a bit of the world.'

Luke decided they'd catch the 2.15 on the Friday. Nia duly drove them to Machynlleth in the Rover. As she dropped them off, she made to press something into Glyn's hand. As soon as he saw the banknotes, Glyn tried to withdraw it.

'Go to a show,' she said. 'On me. I'd like that. Luke would never think of it. He'll lounge around the whole time if you let him.' She pecked him on the cheek. 'You're a good friend for him to have.'

Glyn felt he had no option but to pocket the money, which he did a little guiltily.

The time he'd gone up to London with the school it had been a steam engine. This time a rather sleek new green diesel pulled into the small stone station, and they managed to get a compartment to themselves. Glyn was slightly alarmed at the way the train rocked from side to side. But a glance over at Luke, lounging in the corner with one long leg stretched out on the seat and a cigarette dangling from his mouth, reassured Glyn that this was perfectly normal. Luke began to outline the agenda.

'Brown's tonight I think. It's a club in Frith Street. You'll love it. Maybe some of the gang will be there. Then perhaps lunch somewhere on the river tomorrow, a quick siesta, and then dancing tomorrow night – we'll see where it's at. Bit of a lie in Sunday morning, brunch in Soho, and then amble back late afternoon. That suit?'

'Sounds fine,' said Glyn, vaguely regretting that there were no sights, or the odd museum mentioned. Or even the opera. Glyn's family liked the opera, and often went when a tour came to Aberystwyth. His brother Tom sang in the local male voice choir and would often belt out popular arias around the cowsheds.

'What about a show?'

'A show? Now what on earth would you be interested in seeing?'

'I dunno. We could look into it. Your Mam gave me some money.'

'Oh, bugger that. It'll get us a slap-up meal at Annabel's,' he said, rubbing his hands together.

As the train rattled into Euston it was raining, not the kind of evening that shows the city off to its best. Luke made straight for the taxi rank and hopped into the first one.

'Soho Square please, Squire,' he said, throwing his case on the floor and flopping down into the seat.

Glyn couldn't help staring excitedly out at the people and buildings as the taxi sped down Euston Road, but didn't reveal to Luke that this was his first ride in a London cab. He was conscious of not appearing too much the farm boy. He couldn't remember much about the school trip, so everything was new to him. Even people waiting at bus stops, as tired as they looked at the end of the week, represented a world of glamour for him. He saw them going home to rather swish flats, maybe going out for dinner in their favourite little restaurants around the corner. It was an unknown world to him, one he'd only glimpsed in films. Luke was concentrating on the itinerary.

'That's right, left down Gower Street, right into Oxford Street, and Bob's your uncle.'

'I know the way to Soho Square, Guv,' said the driver with a curt nod.

The rain was coming down heavily when they pulled up.

'Well, at least it's good for business", said Luke as he pulled out his money to pay the driver

'Nah, people either stay at home or go in their own cars,' said the cabbie. 'There's nothing better than the dry shilling.'

Stockton's flat was on the first floor of an elegant Georgian house on the Frith Street corner of the square. It had a large living room with two long shuttered windows facing out onto it. It was very much in the style of the study at Glanharan: green walls, leather chairs, lots of books. There was rather an old-fashioned kitchen with a round table and four chairs, a white-tiled bathroom with shower and bidet, the master bedroom and a smaller bedroom with a single bed.

'You mind bunking down here? I think Stockton would prefer it if I had his room. A quick wash and brush up, then off to Brown's.'

The window of the little study gave on to a courtyard, surrounded by other flats, lights on here and there, a couple of curtains undrawn to reveal people moving around, doing ordinary things like putting a record on or pouring a glass of wine. It reminded Glyn of Hitchcock's Rear Window, adventure waiting to happen somewhere among the different lives that it revealed.

'Christ, surely we can find you something a little more entertaining,' said Luke as Glyn stood there transfixed. 'Come on.'

The club was in a basement just a few minutes' walk away in Frith Street, the entrance at the bottom of the old servants' steps. Sitting at a small desk just inside the door was a long-haired man with thick black-rimmed glasses and a French cigarette between his lips. Luke signed the book and handed over the small charge for guests.

It was a series of rather small rooms leading off each other, with flagstone floors and panelling painted greyish-green. People lounged about in groups on benches at wooden tables, drinking wine and beer.

'Bit different from the Mucky Duck, eh?' said Luke, watching Glyn observing the scene. 'Let's push the boat out and have a bottle of Claret.'

He marched up to the bar, selected the wine unhesitatingly and ushered Glyn to an empty table near the enormous fireplace. They were given glass tumblers for the wine that reminded Glyn of those in his school canteen.

'We can order some food and get it out of the way,' said Luke. 'It's plain, school-type grub but good and cheap and plenty of it.'

They both had huge plates of bangers, mash and onion gravy which Luke bolted down in his usual way, swigged back a whole tumbler of wine and leant back against the wall to see what the evening would bring.

Presently a young man dressed all in black sauntered over with a leggy blond in knee-high red leather boots.

'Luke, you old bastard,' he said, shuffling onto the bench and patting the space next to him for the girl. 'Thought you were buried in darkest Wales or somewhere.'

'Oh, up for the weekend to refuel, dear heart. My friend Glyn,' said Luke, giving a rather theatrical flourish of his hand, 'a real-life native but understands most of what you say to him. Glyn, this is an old Oxford compadre, Piers, and, ah.....?' looking at the girl.

'Laura,' she said.

'Charmed, Laura,' said Luke, leaning over to shake her hand. 'So what mischief are you up to, you old reprobate?'

Piers was working in a car showroom, hoping for something better in the automotive line. Laura helped out in a boutique on the King's Road, awaiting her break into modelling.

'Wales sounds so quaint,' said Laura, looking at Glyn. 'You must tell me all about it.'

Glyn didn't know where to begin.

'Well, I live on a farm,' he said.

'Oh, that's too sweet for words. I've always wanted to live on a farm.'

Glyn couldn't suppress a smile as he tried to picture her in wellies mucking out the cowshed.

'Where did you go to school?' she asked.

'Oh, I just went to the local high school,' said Glyn.

'Oh,' she said, and looked slightly confused.

Glyn couldn't help liking her although it was becoming all too obvious that they had very little in common. She was attractive and had a kind face. She was smoking long, pastel-coloured cigarettes and offered Glyn one.

'No, thanks,' he said. 'I'll stick to my Embassies.'

'Embassies! I thought only lorry-drivers and builders smoked those.'

Conversation meandered on, touching on the latest parties, the whereabouts and exploits of mutual friends, the coming weekend's events. Little attention was paid to Glyn, but he was happy enough taking it all in. Not so different from the Mucky Duck in some ways, he thought. A little more parochial if anything, as they showed scant interest in and even less knowledge of the world outside their set. In the Mucky Duck, as well as local gossip and business, there was healthy and often heated debate on politics and the affairs of the day.

Every so often Laura would turn to Glyn and try to include him in the conversation. These efforts consisted largely of enquiries about whether he knew certain people the others were talking about, and of course, he didn't. She couldn't seem to grasp this.

'Oh, you must know Dicky Oliver,' she said, in one final attempt. 'Everyone does.'

'I'm afraid not,' he said. 'This is my first real time in London.'

'Oh,' said Laura, again with that look of confusion.

Two or three others ambled casually up to them in the course of the evening and talk proceeded along similar lines. For all their interesting backgrounds, quite exotic to Glyn, and privileged education, they kept to a fairly easy, carefree banter. They seemed most interested in providing running commentary on their own lives, likes and loves, in stark contrast to the laconic style of Glyn's own world. Their conversation consisted of cheap point-scoring.

'That's a horrible thing to say,' said a young man to the woman sitting next to him - Glyn couldn't tell if they constituted a couple.

'I'm a horrible person – hadn't you realised?' she shot back.

None of them seemed to have any real ambition to do anything worthwhile. In a way it was part of their uniform. It wasn't the in thing to be too enthusiastic about anything that was considered too normal or bourgeois - a word that cropped up often - particularly careers. Glyn was interested to know what they'd done at university, but they were very vague about it and waved any questions away in a bored manner, as did Luke. He could never quite get to the bottom of how exactly Luke did spend his time at Oxford, apart from self-indulgently, and Luke was even vaguer about his future plans. Glyn wasn't quite sure what he was expecting from this graduate group, if anything, but just a little more. He kept waiting for someone to say something interesting. Luke, on the other hand, seemed to be enjoying himself to the full. He was in his natural habitat. Glyn saw that the situation was reversed from the Mucky Duck – now it was he who was the outsider. He thought how difficult life in Aberharan must be for Luke, although he always appeared very much at ease.

The club closed at one o'clock and Luke and Glyn sauntered back to Soho Square. Luke poured them large brandies from a decanter on the drinks tray on the sideboard. Glyn sipped it slowly, although he felt as if he'd had enough. Luke seemed completely incurious as to what Glyn made of his friends, but he said, 'That Laura seemed to take a shine to you. Pity's she's taken.'

They got up late next morning and as there was no food in the flat they had tea and bacon sandwiches in a nearby cafe. It was a beautiful day after the rain and everything seemed fresh and full of life. Passers-by were in a happy, expectant mood, like in the opening shots of a Swinging London film. Glyn still wanted to see some sights, but knew it would probably be useless to suggest it. Luke, as Nia had predicted, showed no interest in anything other than pubs and clubs, but always seemed to have something up his sleeve.

So they made their way to a pub on the river where they had lunch with Piers and Buster, a tall and stocky man in a kaftan who was a drummer in a band, playing gigs in South London pubs. Laura was said to be 'sleeping it off,' which, despite the fact that they had found little common ground, Glyn rather regretted. At least she made an effort to talk to him. As it was, the trio merely continued in the same vein as the previous night, going into fits of laughter at the mere mention of someone's name or some drunken escapade of their past.

Then it was back to the flat for a siesta at about five, in preparation for the night ahead at Annabel's and another club in Tottenham Court Road. At the restaurant Luke held out his hand for Nia's show money and set about ordering some of the most expensive things on the menu and wine list, which he negotiated with his usual aplomb. Luke ordered dishes which again were new to Glyn: foie gras, beef Wellington, Tarte Tatin. All accompanied by quantities of quality wine, and rounded off with cheese and port. Glyn thought he coped with it rather well, managing to take it in his stride and hide his culinary inexperience. But as much as he enjoyed it, he couldn't help thinking that real London life was elsewhere. Then he'd feel guilty and ungrateful. His friend after all was showing him a world he may never otherwise have known.

At the club, Luke mounted a determined and unabashed campaign to get off with someone, and he quickly succeeded. Glyn was somewhat shocked, given the blossoming romance with Sian, but knew it would be distinctly uncool, perhaps even bourgeois, to say anything. As the evening wore on Luke took him aside and asked him if would mind if he brought his dancing partner back to the flat, saying he would see if she had a friend for him. He was about to protest, say something about Sian, but he caught the pleading look in Luke's eyes and he hesitated, not knowing exactly what to say. These people did not seem to pay any heed to the normal rules of loyalty.

As for himself, Glyn felt a little awkward. He was not used to moving so fast with strangers, but did not want to seem a prude. He'd had a couple of girlfriends, and was not the virgin he suspected Luke took him for. It was as if he was playing a game, without knowing the rules himself. He just said he could find his own, thank you, and Luke was to do as he pleased. Luke introduced him to the dancing partner, a small bubbly brunette called Vicky.

It was the early hours when the three of them returned to the flat. Glyn went straight to bed.

They had planned to take the one o'clock train home, but by half past twelve there was no sign of life from the master bedroom. Glyn was furious with his friend, and the growing loyalty he felt towards Luke was being properly tested for the first time. He briefly considered making his own way to Euston, but he'd have to ring home for a lift from the station, and there'd have to be explanations to his mother and Nia, not to mention Sian. He decided in the end to make use of the afternoon and catch the later train.

He left a note saying he'd be back around five, and walked down through Piccadilly Circus and Trafalgar Square to Westminster where he saw the Houses of Parliament and the Abbey, then down the Mall to Buckingham Palace and back. He was struck by the throngs of people, all of them seeming to have a sense of purpose, even of urgency, as they hurried along.

On his return he found Luke and Vicky lolling on the sofa listening to records, smoking cigarettes and drinking mugs of black coffee. It was four o'clock and Glyn thought they'd be in time to catch the last train at six.

'Oh there you are,' said Luke. 'What say we stay an extra night?' he asked Glyn. 'We could get the early train back tomorrow and Ma'll be sober enough to pick us up from the station.'

Glyn was angry with both of them, but didn't know what to say, or how to say it without losing his rage completely. Vicky glanced up at him expectantly. She certainly looked at home, lying in Luke's arms. Glyn rang home. His mother, as he dreaded, answered in her phone voice and carefully gave the number. He made up some story about Luke having to stay on to meet a relative that night.

'Having that good a time, are you?' asked his mother curtly. 'Oh, well, we'll see you when we see you. I'll tell Dad. I'm sure they'll manage. Somehow.'

Luke and Vicky seemed disinclined to move from the sofa, so Glyn spent the evening taking another walk, this time around the streets of Soho, drinking it all in, feeling quite worldly. At least he'd had a chance to see something of the city.

On the train back the next morning, Luke dozed comfortably in the corner of his window seat. Vicky had stayed the night again, and had got up early to go and change before she went to work. She made Glyn a cup of coffee and told him she was a nurse. She was pleasant enough. Glyn wondered vaguely what her parents would make of her stopping out for the weekend. But then he told himself he was being a country bumpkin. She probably lived in a nurse's home, led her own life. He could barely bring himself to be civil to Luke and they'd hardly exchanged a word. Luke, in something of a dreamy state, seemed oblivious.

As the countryside sped past, he looked at Luke dozing in the opposite corner. Even with his face distorted as he slumped against the window, the tip of his tongue protruding slightly and gentle snores emanating from his nose, he still managed to look debonair.

But some of his glow had, for Glyn, already paled. Could friendship blossom and fade so quickly? All of his other friends he had known most, if not all, of his life. But then, Luke was different.

Glyn reflected on the weekend. He had loved it in some ways. It had both met and fallen short of his expectations of the glamorous life. Luke seemed, he couldn't avoid the word, shallow at times. It was clear that he'd had one objective for the weekend and that was sex. He wondered now if Luke had even asked Sian to come, whether it wasn't a lie to hide the plan he'd had all along. A part of him was disgusted with Luke's behaviour but another part, maybe larger, still admired his worldly ways, envied even. He could suddenly surprise you with a perceptive, intelligent remark. And as much as he seemed to care about anyone, he seemed to care about Glyn. Indeed, as popular as Luke seemed with his own crowd, they seemed to be more acquaintances than friends. He could drift as easily out of their lives as he drifted in. They didn't seem to have the solid basis of comradeship that Glyn had with Johnny Jones, for example, even if he had been neglecting him a little of late. But what of Sian? It was because of her that Glyn didn't know if he'd ever be able to fully forgive him.

And there was a deeper sense of disappointment with his introduction to those aimless London graduates. They were hardly a good advertisement for the city university life that had been luring him away from the farm. Did he really want to be part of it? Was it worth leaving home for? No, he'd have to think again. And now, was there also something - or someone - keeping him in Mid-Wales?

Nia was on the platform to meet them, in headscarf and sunglasses, her arms folded and a cigarette poised in her right hand. On the way back she questioned Luke about the time they'd had. He gave the barest of outlines.

'What about you, Glyn? How did you find life in Soho?'

'Oh, grand,' said Glyn.

'What about your mother? Did she mind you stopping over an extra day? Did the cows manage to get milked?' Again that quick glance in the mirror at Glyn in the back, a slightly mischievous smile playing on her lips. Glyn smiled himself.

'What shows did you see?' she asked of the mirror.

'Nothing worth seeing,' said Luke to the passenger window. 'And we had loads of people to catch up with.'

When they reached the end of Bryngwanwyn lane Glyn insisted they dropped him off at the bottom, although Nia wanted to take him up to the house.

Glyn hopped out quickly. Luke gave him a brief, salute-like wave through the window, still in his own dreamy world. He stood for a moment, seeing the car speed off, but his attention was elsewhere. There was something wrong, something not as it should be, but he couldn't put his finger on it. And then he realised what it was. Something wasn't there that usually was: there were no churns on the milk stand. He walked up the lane, his old canvas knapsack on his back, wondering what could have happened. As he rounded the first bend he could see the white bed sheets flapping on the clothesline at the side of the house in the orchard. Monday, washday, was a busy one for his mother and Nain.

It was another sunny day, but some dark blue clouds were loitering over the hills. The smoke curled up from the kitchen chimney. He could smell fresh creosote on the gates on the lane - his father's job. From the woods down below came the plaintive caw of wood pigeons, and cows lowed in the Field By The House as they waited to be milked. As he came into the yard he saw Tom sharpening the blades on the mower ready for the hay harvest.

[handwritten marginal edits, partly legible: "working on the baler ... kneeling tinkering with the innards of the baler, an oil can with a very long spout ... perched precariously on the top above his head. On Peary's foot ... he got up and wiped his head ... oven acting"]

'Hullo, city boy. They didn't keep you there then?' he shouted.

Glyn walked over towards him.

'What's happened to the milk churns?'

'Ha! You've forgotten already. You *are* turning into a city boy.'

'What?'

'The new milk tank came Saturday. Come and have a look.'

Tom led him to the room at the end of the cowshed they called the dairy, where the milk churns were kept. Tom unlatched the door and inside, instead, was a large square tank of gleaming stainless steel. Tom lifted one of the lids. It was half full of milk, being slowly stirred by a metal paddle.

'It's refrigerated, look. No more warm milk. Here, have a taste.'

Tom took an enamel jug from the window ledge, dipped it into the milk and proffered it to his brother. Glyn drank from the jug.

'Lovely,' he said.

He and his brothers had always hated the warm milk that came from the cows and had always waited for it to cool in pantry.

Glyn had indeed forgotten that they were having the tank. It meant one more chore had disappeared from the farm work - the daily carting of the full milk churns to the stand at the bottom of the lane, and the carting back of the empty ones the milk lorry replaced them with. Now, a tanker would come up to the farm and pipe the milk straight in. It would mean a lot less work for Tom. No wonder he look so pleased with it. He'd always been the mechanic of the family - their father was hopeless - and had studied engineering at the Tech. It was Tom who forced the pace of modern machinery, who made sure that they had the latest labour-saving equipment. Yet it had always been assumed that if anyone left the farm, it would be Glyn. He wondered now if this was unfair, especially with his new-found misgivings about university life. Maybe he should talk it over with Tom. He finished the milk. Tom had already gone about his work.

He continued up to the front of the house where he could see his mother sitting at the table on the small patch of grass, shelling peas. The grass had been mown and the delicious aroma mixed with that of the creosote and wood smoke. He slung down his knapsack and sat down on the wooden bench opposite his mother. They said hello but nothing else for a good minute. He could see his mother was itching to know about the weekend, perhaps searching for the right way of getting some information without giving her approval by showing too much curiosity. But Glyn could be as tight-lipped as she could.

'You survived it then?' she came out with eventually, peas pinging into the colander.

'Yeah, it wasn't too bad. Quite interesting really. But they can be a funny old lot,' he said. Perhaps he felt he ought to make some concession to the prejudice he perceived in his mother.

'Well, ah. Could've told you that myself without you going to the expense of going there. Still, these places are there to see, I suppose. How did you get back from Machynlleth?'

'Nia came to fetch us.'

'Nia now, is it?'

'Well, what else do you want me to call her?'

'I could think of one or two things,' she said, concentrating on the peas.

This was a bit much, even for his mother. So their afternoon tea together had done little to soften her attitude to Nia in the long term. If anything, it seemed to have hardened it.

She picked up the colander of peas. 'Go and chuck those shells in the pigsty,' she said, 'I've still got the beds to make,' and went inside the house.

8

And so sultry summer mellowed into a crisp, smoky autumn. The swallows gathered on the telephone wires and in an instant were gone. The woods between Bryngwanwyn and Glanharan blazed with red and copper so vivid that it seemed impossible that the trees would soon be bare. The lanes started to swirl with leaves like shoals of fish which seemed to obey a synchronised dance of their own.

For a while after the London trip, Glyn was busy in the corn harvest and didn't hear from his friend. He avoided the Mucky Duck and went instead to the Aberharan Hotel with his brothers after a busy week in the cornfield. He imagined that Luke was spending more time with Sian, and he was glad that he was being left alone.

About three weeks after the trip a call came from Luke. He and Sian were going to the Mucky Duck and wanted Glyn to join them. He could hardly refuse, and he was certainly looking forward to seeing Sian again. London wasn't mentioned.

She seemed pleased to see him too. When she went to the loo, Luke announced out of the blue that he was going to ask Sian to marry him. This was the last thing Glyn was expecting, and he couldn't muster the congratulatory enthusiasm that he felt was in order.

'Well, what do you think?' Luke asked, a little put out perhaps that his announcement had been greeted in silence.

'What will she think?'

'I mean, do you think I should ask her?'

'How serious are you about it?'

'Well....serious! Why else should I be asking you?'

'Dunno. I didn't know you were thinking about settling down.'

'Exactly. I wasn't. That's how come I know.'

'Know what?'

'Know I should ask her....'

This called for some coded speaking, Glyn decided.

'Are you sure you're ready for.....well, monogamy?' he asked.

'Look, Glyn,' said Luke, leaning forward with his elbows on the table and keeping one eye on the passage that led to the toilets, 'that meant nothing. It was just a fling, a last fling. I knew I was getting serious on Sian and it just helped me make up my mind. You can't blame a bloke.'

Indeed, he didn't know whether he could, or should, blame Luke – he had that way of making his behaviours sound reasonable, commendable even. Perhaps Glyn was just being a prude after all.

Sian returned. The two young men both launched into small talk at the same time to mask the conversation they'd just had. Sian sensed that something was in the air.

'What's up?' she asked. 'You two had a tiff?'

The pair laughed it off as best they could, but the evening didn't quite regain its conviviality. No more was said about a proposal, but as Glyn walked up Bryngwanwyn lane, he realised he didn't want Luke to marry Sian and the main reason, he told himself, was that he didn't think Luke would make her a good husband. They made a fine pair, but he couldn't see it being a happy marriage. He wondered if there was anything he could do to stop it.

Next Saturday in the early evening Glyn got a call at the farm. He was in the Meal House, where they kept food for the animals, emptying meal into the big wooden bins.

'Phone!' shouted his mother down the yard. It was just a moment or two after Glyn had heard the outside bell ring, so she hadn't spent much time chatting. She managed to convey in that one yelled word that she didn't quite approve of the caller, so odds on it was Glanharan.

'Don't go down the pub, come here ASAP,' said Luke with his customary lack of preamble, and put the phone down.

Half-intrigued and half-annoyed at the peremptory summons, Glyn washed and changed and set off down the path through the woods with a torch. Lights were blazing as he reached the house and the back door was open, even in the bitter cold. Sounds of merrymaking came to greet him. Glyn felt a lurch in his stomach and braced himself. There were still times, especially when Nia had been drinking, when he felt out of his depth at Glanharan, unsure of himself. Yet its whole aura had for him an undeniable allure.

They were all in the kitchen sitting round the table. Stockton and Briddy were both down for the weekend, nursing drinks while Nia and Luke were fairly swilling them back.

'Ah, Glyn,' said Nia, stretching out a majestic hand. 'Great timing. We're going to have a New Year's party. A grand one, all the trimmings. A catered affair. Everyone will be invited.' She swept her hand rather haphazardly around her.

'What do you think, Glyn?' asked Stockton. 'How will the natives react to Nia playing lady of the manor?'

Glyn had not got over his initial dislike of Stockton, although he had half-heartedly tried. He didn't say much - maybe it was hard for him to get a word in edgeways - but often when he did he always seemed to hit some kind of uncomfortable note.

'Well, I don't know.' He glanced at Luke who seemed to be weighing up the idea himself. 'People round here don't like anything too showy.'

'Poppycock,' said Nia with a shake of her head, dismissing any dissension in the ranks. Glyn liked the word, and the way she said it. It was a word no-one else he knew would ever say, and called for white teeth and painted red lips. 'Don't forget I know them better than you do. They may pretend to get embarrassed by a good show and complain that it's a lot of fuss, but deep down they love it. Look at all the hunt balls and Young Farmers' dinners and things. The ladies love dressing up. The men needn't wear black ties if they don't want to.'

'Quite as well,' said Stockton. 'It's a bit of a tall order after a hard day in the fields.'

'Stockton, you have a very Hollywood notion of life in rural Britain,' said Nia. 'You Americans think you're so classless but you're positively feudal. Don't you realise this will be a very democratic affair? We'll have everyone down from London too.' She glanced around the room. 'It's about time we showed the old place off.'

She squeezed Briddy's hand. 'What fun we'll have planning it all.'

Briddy sipped her wine and looked as if she'd have more fun planning her own funeral.

'Let's go next door,' said Nia getting up unsteadily.

'Why? We don't even know them,' said Stockton in a rare attempt at a joke.

Nia ignored him. 'It's ridiculous how much time we spend in the kitchen. I want to start mapping the whole thing out in my mind in comfort in the lounge.'

Stockton and Briddy followed her with an air of resignation.

'Come along, boys,' shouted Nia over her shoulder.

But Luke poured himself another scotch and seemed to want to linger in the kitchen.

'So what do you make of this party idea?' Glyn asked Luke. He himself had misgivings which he couldn't quite put his finger on.

'Could be fun, as long as Ma doesn't go overboard. We'll have to rein her in. But Sian might like it. We could announce our engagement. We could surprise Ma. Not upstage her though, that would be fatal.'

Glyn shot Luke a glance. He was hunched over the table, both hands round his tumbler, sucking on his scotch, inscrutable.

'So you've popped the question, then?'

'I've mooted the possibility, yes. She seems quite keen on the idea.' He looked like a small boy who's just got the toy he wanted for Christmas.

'Is that why you asked me down here?'

'Well, yes.....'

'I thought it was a matter of national importance, or something.'

'It is,' said Luke, banging his fist on the table. 'It's my entire future.'

'Aren't you a bit young?'

'I'm twenty-three,' said Luke, with a defiant thrust of his chin.

'Exactly,' said Glyn. 'And you haven't even got a job. Have you thought about how you'd keep her? Where'd you live?'

'Oh Glyn, don't be so bourgeois.' Glyn held back from pointing out that the word could hardly be applied to him. 'True love finds a way,' went on Luke. 'This is 1969. I don't have to keep her. She can keep herself. And anyway, we're only talking about getting engaged. I haven't even thought about marriage yet'

'Why are you so bothered about getting engaged then?'

'I don't know. I don't want to lose her. I've never felt this way about anyone and I know I never will again. She's the one, Glyn.'

'Well, you seem to have made your mind up.'

'Well, yes, but I wanted the chance to talk it over with me old mate.'

As so often, Glyn could not tell whether he was being facetious or not. He seemed reluctant to join the others and, unusually, they were not summoned by Nia. When Glyn went through to the lounge to say goodnight, she was slumped over the end of the sofa, half-asleep, with a girlish grin on her face. Briddy looked guilty, and Stockton looked grumpy.

'I was about to make some coffee,' said Briddy, getting up and glancing swiftly at Stockton.

Glyn said he had to be going. After the earlier promise, the evening had fizzled out somewhat.

On his way back up through the silent woods. Glyn tried to sort out his feelings about the party, the surprise announcement of the engagement. He'd have to be there, of course. But there was the worry about having his entire family on display at Glanharan, if indeed they'd come. He thought they probably would at the last minute, after a lot of grumbling to show they weren't in the thrall of their glamorous neighbours. And there was also the worry about having Nia on display to his entire family. Would she behave herself, stay sober enough to be charming? Glamour was best viewed from afar, as Nia herself acknowledged. So far the brief meetings of the two worlds had gone off reasonably well, but not without a certain awkwardness. Did he want his two worlds to become one? Was it possible?

He was aware too that there were other emotions in his reaction. A lightness of excitement, for sure. But a heaviness too, which went beyond the anxiety about the colliding worlds. Luke was exotic and dull at the same time, giving the impression of wit and worldliness. It was like waiting for a brightly-coloured parrot to say something surprising. In the recesses of his mind maybe he had an inkling of what this heaviness was, but scarcely wanted to think it. No, he couldn't be jealous. Of what? Of whom? He tried to bring some order into the confusion of his thoughts. What he couldn't quite work out was whether this was because he thought Luke was rushing into things too quickly, or because he was being drawn to Sian more and more himself. And then there was something else. Nia had taken her under her wing, as at first she had Glyn, and now had little time for anyone else when she was around. They seemed natural together, Nia taking Sian gently in her arm when she arrived at Glanharan, walking her around the garden. At these times Nia seemed at her best, her most serene. At other times Glyn was shocked at Nia's state when he came back to the house after a night in the pub with Luke. Glyn was aware that she rarely behaved as badly when Stockton or Briddy were around. But when they weren't, she seemed to let herself go, and increasingly not to care much for anyone around her. Then she'd withdraw from those intimate, whispered conversations that Glyn had come to enjoy so much. They made him feel grown-up, and, though he would hardly admit it to himself, sexual.

She was still perfectly friendly to Glyn, but he missed those early days when he'd had her to himself, when she treated him as an equal, an intimate. In some ways then, he was jealous both of Luke and Sian. But which was the stronger?

Late in November Luke turned up for pack drill at the Mucky Duck on a Saturday evening, had a couple of drinks with Glyn and company at the bar, then motioned to Glyn that he wanted to go and sit by the fire, even though he knew by now this was against protocol this early on in the evening. But the friends had got to know Luke and tended to be lenient towards his breaches of the rules.

'Sian wants to go and see a play in Aberystwyth next week. It's a French play, but in English, called something like Hippopotamus, by someone called Unesco. Isn't that something to do with the United Nations?'

'Ionesco,' said Glyn, stabbing a little in the dark. He was pretty sure he had heard of him, and although he couldn't have said much about him, enjoyed showing off knowledge to his worldly friend.

'You see, that's why I need you along, so I don't make a total tit of myself.'

'OK, I'll come, but I don't know much more about him than you. Probably.'

'That's decided then,' said Luke, slapping him on the leg in a way that Glyn still found embarrassing, and couldn't help glancing around to see if anyone was looking.

Glyn looked up Ionesco the next day in the encyclopaedia of literature he'd got for English A level. He found that he was a prime exponent of The Theatre of the Absurd, which he found intriguing, and that Luke probably meant a play called Rhinoceros. It was about the need to conform and follow the crowd. Maybe it would be quite an enjoyable outing after all. He hadn't seen Sian for a while.

Luke was meant to drive and pick Sian up on the way, but when the day came there was a light covering of snow and more forecast. In the afternoon Luke rang Bryngwanwyn and told Glyn he didn't think the old Rover was up to it.

'Do you think your Pa will let you have the Land Rover?' he asked.

Glyn didn't want to have to ask, but he couldn't see another way. He knew this was important to Luke. In the event his father said yes, as long as he was careful. His mother looked on in disapproval, but said nothing. Glyn picked up Luke at Glanharan, and directed him to Sian's small terraced house in Llanfair. The roads had been gritted and were fairly clear most of the way, with just a few dicey patches on the mountain road to

Aberystwyth. Glyn enjoyed driving. It made him feel important, useful, and not the gooseberry he often felt when he was with Luke and Sian.

The play was in the university theatre and Sian sat between them.

'One leg each,' quipped Luke as they took their places. Glyn's eyes met Sian's briefly and he noticed a slight look of alarm. He wondered what she could see in his.

She was as absorbed in the play as Glyn was. But he could tell Luke the other side was distracted and Sian had to keep whispering to him to shut up. Afterwards they piled in together on the front bench of the Land Rover.

'You don't mind if I cwtch up?' Sian said to Glyn. 'It's so cold. Doesn't the heater work in this old thing?'

'Not many mod cons left, I'm afraid,' said Glyn, as he revved up the Land Rover with a roar from its old exhaust. 'It's army surplus and years old, but a trusty steed at that.'

'Come on, Luke, snuggle up,' said Sian. 'It's our only chance of getting warm.'

'What's this cootch business?' asked Luke.

'It means a snuggle,' said Sian. 'It's what you ask your Mam for when you're little. "Can I have a cwtch?"'

Luke gave a little snort and lit up a cigarette. He was not in a good mood, and it was all the more noticeable because he was usually so easy-going. Sian glanced at Glyn in the flickering lights as they headed up the hill out of the town. They smiled at each other and Sian started off again about the play. Glyn wondered if she knew this would merely annoy Luke even more, or if she cared, or if she wanted it this way.

'I did the play at Bangor,' she said. Her rare references to university life were a far cry from the irreverence of the London lot: for her it had been an important, mind-expanding part of her life. 'I love Ionesco. But do you think he's saying it's inevitable that we all want to fit in with the crowd, even when it's Nazism or something, or do we have a choice?'

'I suppose he's saying it takes a lot of strength to resist, when everyone else condemns you for not conforming.'

Luke was unusually quiet and seemed on edge. He leant against the door in a carefully nonchalant manner and drummed his fingers on the metal dashboard. He kept glancing at his watch and when they came to the next roadside pub he suggested they'd just make it for last orders. But it had started snowing again and while the gritters had been out on the main road again, when they came to the turn-off to Sian's village, a sharp left up a hill, they saw it was thick with clean snow.

'We'd better press on,' said Glyn, 'or we might not make it back tonight.'

'You'll have to come back to Glanharan with us,' said Luke in a tone that brooked no argument. 'Straight on, driver.'

Sian nudged Glyn in his ribs and he had to turn a snigger into a cough. He was dimly aware that by drawing him into conspiratorial closeness, emphasising their Welshness and discussing the play in which Luke had shown little interest, she was teasing Luke. Or was it something different from teasing? Glyn didn't care. It felt nice. And he had far more in common with her than Luke did. He wondered how aware she was of this, and whether it mattered. He could feel her snuggling up to him. Luke was still slouched against the passenger window. Glyn sensed that there was something growing between him and Sian. Yet it was impossible: surely she was beyond his reach – off limits. And then there was Luke....

Glyn made his way slowly up the hill. The snow was now coming down on the windscreen faster than the feeble wipers could clear it. The going was slow and traffic was backing up on the twisting road. At times Glyn almost had to stop, and a couple of times the old Land Rover went into a slow, majestic skid, but Glyn managed to right it in time. He had neglected to put the chains around the tyres.

The trio lapsed into an uneasy silence, each absorbed in thought. They were all mindful that to the right was an almost vertical drop and there were no hedges on this part of the road. Glyn drove as carefully as he could, but knew that slow driving was no guarantee against the hazards of the journey. He was aware of his two friends and the responsibility he had for getting them home. It called for resolution, for gentle but firm feet on the pedals. He thought too of Nia, waiting for them, and some part of him wanted to get back to her.

It was very late when they reached Glanharan. Luke hopped out with a sigh of relief and helped Sian down.

'You'd better come in and stay too,' he called to Glyn as they ran to the door.

Glyn had to concede that by now the Land Rover would probably not make it up Bryngwanwyn lane and he didn't fancy walking it. He parked it in one of the garages opposite the back door and ran inside himself. They shook off their coats and left them in the hall with their shoes. They found Nia alone in the lounge listening to Billie Holiday on the record player – *Feelin' Good*. These were her staples – Billie, Ella, Nat King Cole, Louis Armstrong. Music Glyn had barely heard, but he would forever associate it with those drunken evenings with Nia at Glanharan. She was nursing a vodka martini in a cocktail glass with its hallmark small silver onion. She seemed to be in a delicately-balanced mood, mellow rather than melodramatic, but one which could easily tip over if she had one too many martinis.

'Ah, there you are. Good. Sian, so glad you came. Luke, brandies all round, I think. You all look as if you could do with it.'

Glyn reflected that time at Glanharan obeyed no normal laws. If they arrived home this late at his home it would be straight to bed. He didn't even see the point of phoning home to tell them where he was. They'd all be asleep.

Nia kissed Sian on the cheek and patted a place next to her on the sofa.

'Now, what was the play? Rhinoceros? Ah, Ionesco. How nice'

Glyn wouldn't have thought you could describe Ionesco as nice and was never quite sure how much Nia really knew about theatre.

'He was right,' she was saying. 'It is difficult in life not to follow the herd. Now, I want to discuss the New Year's party.'

In the absence of Stockton and Briddy that weekend Nia was clearly entertaining herself by giving unfettered flight to her fancies.

'I was thinking just wines and champagne, punches and eggnog. Wet bar, canapes handed round on silver salvers....'

'Now hang on a mo, Ma,' said Luke. 'If you want everyone to come and actually enjoy themselves you'd better give them what they want instead of scripting a movie do.'

He seemed to have perked up again now that he was back in his natural habitat. If that was the right phrase. Cynefin, it would be in Welsh, the patch of ground where sheep felt at home. It was one of those words that Welsh-speakers like to think had no real equivalent in English.

'Oh, they can have what they want the rest of the year.' She waved aside the comment instinctively, but then gave a start as it struck home.

'What do they want?' she demanded, swinging around to Glyn.

'Well, I suppose the men will want beer and whisky. They're not too impressed with a buffet at the best of times. A knife and fork dinner is more their idea of pushing the boat out. And what's a wet bar when it's at home?'

'Oh, you know, shellfish - oysters and things on crushed ice. Sian, you're always so practical in these matters, what do you think?'

Sian thought Nia could strike a good working compromise between a more traditional cold meats buffet and her own stylish flourishes. Nia reluctantly accepted that she would have to bow, slightly but gracefully, to local custom. She promised to tone down the proceedings and listen to her Council of War in Luke, Sian and Glyn.

'Come, on darling. Let's go up to bed,' said Luke. 'I'm exhausted.'

'Sian, you're in the spare room next to mine,' said Nia sharply, emphasising the last three words. Glyn noticed Luke give Nia a glance of annoyance. He guessed there had been some prior discussion about this, which Luke had lost. Sleeping arrangements clearly fell into the category of things Nia was strict about.

Sian smiled goodnight at them both, and Luke put his arm around her and ushered her out of the room proprietorially.

'You can sleep in the room at the top of the stairs,' said Nia to Glyn, pouring him another large brandy which he didn't want. 'When you're ready' she added, which Glyn interpreted as 'When I'm ready.'

She hesitated slightly before handing him the glass, marshalling her thoughts.

'You're probably asking yourself what I'm doing, playing the lady of the manor like this, throwing swanky parties for the peasants. No,' she held up her hand to forestall Glyn's protest, 'I know you're thinking that, and a lot more people will. But I don't care. It's what I've been waiting for.'

'What do you mean, waiting for?'

Nia took a long gulp, smacked her lips and caressed her glass.

'Even though I was just a two bit actress, people think I have everything. Been to Hollywood, made a lot of money. And so I have. But contrary to common credence you don't reach a plateau of happiness and stay there. Happiness comes in small packages. If you're lucky there are moments of contentment, but on the whole they're fleeting. You can't catch them, hold them, keep them. It's what makes us human. We're always waiting for something - the right person, marriage, kids, a good job, a better job. And so it goes on. I was very lucky, I know. But it still wasn't enough. And that's hard to explain to people who think you have it all, who envy you. You're not to complain. I had to find this next thing. And this was it. Coming home. And it isn't easy, believe you me. Few things that are worth it are. But it's what I've been waiting for. Perhaps one day I'll tell you why. If you really want to get to the heart of a person, ask them what they're waiting for.'

She took another greedy gulp of her vodka and looked admiringly at the glass.

'"Slow Curtain",' she quoted. '"The End".'

As he drifted off to sleep in the room decorated entirely in yellow and white, Glyn had a flash of comprehension about what it was he had been waiting for. As much as he loved his family and the farm, it was to go away and make his own way in the world. There was now no doubt. He made up his mind to tell his parents the very next day.

But when he got home in the morning, driving in the tracks on the lane already made by the tractor, he found his father sitting alone in the kitchen. It was quiet, without the usual bustle. His father looked shaken.

'Your Nain's been taken ill,' he said on seeing Glyn. 'Your mother's up with her now.'

Glyn went straight up, forgetting his prepared speeches.

9

When he opened the door to Nain's room he got a shock. She was sitting up in bed, and his mother was putting a clean nightdress on her. It wasn't so much her bare breasts that shocked him, but the long white hair cascading down her shoulders. He had never seen her with her hair down, in any sense of the phrase. In fact he always thought of her with short hair. He lingered at the door with his hand on the knob.

'Come in, if you're going to,' said his mother wearily.

Nain looked at him with something approaching alarm.

'Dyma fe, yn ol,' she whispered to his mother. He's come back.

'Why'd she say that?' asked Glyn.

'Oh, she isn't making much sense about anything.'

He waited until his mother had finished, and they walked slowly down the stairs. His Nain had had a stroke the previous evening, falling from her chair at the table.

'Is she going to get better?' asked Glyn.

'I don't think so, Glyn. She's eighty-five. They don't often recover at that age.'

'Are you OK?'

'Me? Oh, yes, I'll survive. It's just when they reach a certain age you think they're going to go on forever. Silly, isn't it?'

For the next three weeks his mother spent most of the time caring for her. His father and brothers mucked in as best they could, cooking and doing the washing up, although it was no surprise for his sons to learn that their father could not even make a cup of coffee. In the evenings Glyn would sometimes sit with his mother and Nain for an hour, feeling useless but sensing that his mother liked him there. Nain said next to nothing, tried to mumble a few words now and again. Several times she stared at Glyn with that same look of alarm, and mentioned something about him coming back. But much of the time she wept quietly to herself, as if she realised that after a life of hard work, it had come to this.

In the end she slipped quietly away. Glyn and his mother were with her. She looked peaceful at last. His mother busied herself with arrangements for the funeral. Extra gin would have to be brought in for Auntie Blod. A fine spread would have to be provided. Glyn's mother told him of the time when she was taken into the parlour to see her own grandmother laid out. In those days the coffin stayed in the house until the funeral, and only the men went to the chapel.

Luke rang to offer his condolences.

'Should we come to the funeral?' he asked.

'Well, thanks, but there's no need at all,' said Glyn. It was the last thing he wanted, and Luke sounded relieved. 'You didn't really know her. There'll be plenty of people there. But thanks for the thought.'

The little chapel was indeed packed out for the funeral, as always in the farming world a great social occasion, especially for someone so well-known. Johnny Jones and his family were there, which meant a lot to Glyn. They came back to Bryngwanwyn for the do afterwards. Auntie Blod soon dried her tears and before long was leading everyone in the Hokey Kokey.

Meanwhile, plans for the Glanharan party were going ahead. Life went on. All kinds of unfamiliar delivery vans bounced up the drive to unload hampers and cases of wine and champagne. The poultry was coming from Bryngwanwyn. Glyn's mother reared turkeys and geese at this time of year for the family, and to sell for her Christmas purse as she called it. Once Nia heard this, she put in an order. She also commissioned Luke and Glyn to take care of the beer, which they did simply enough by ordering kegs from Ed one night in the Mucky Duck.

What with his grandmother's illness and funeral, and the busy approach of Christmas, it was about the one time Glyn had seen Luke for weeks. And as they sat at their table in the bar, everything was as it used to be, save for a certain tension between them. Even Luke, for the first time since Glyn had known him, seemed lost for something to say. Maybe the friendship was running to the end of its course. Maybe he didn't belong in their world after all. But another possibility struck Glyn forcefully in one of the silences. Could Luke resent the growing closeness, as Glyn perceived it, between him and Sian? It was curious that he didn't mention her, didn't even reveal whether they were going ahead with the engagement. Glyn wanted to know, but couldn't bring himself to ask. They parted with rather perfunctory cheerios. It had been an unsatisfactory night for Glyn, probably for both of them.

But Glanharan still made its presence felt in Glyn's old, familiar world. Embossed invitation cards to the New Year's Eve party started dropping through the letter boxes of the village and being handed over at the farmhouse doors surrounding it. Excitement and anticipation stirred behind masks of nonchalance, and Nia's party became an unavoidable topic of conversation.

In the barn at Bryngwanwyn, Glyn, his mother, father and Alun sat on hay bales feathering turkeys. Every available hand was required to feather and dress them. It was mind-numbing, not to say thumb-numbing, work which passed all the more quickly if there was something good to talk about. Glyn never looked forward to the feathering, but enjoyed it in a way when the time came. For as long as he could remember it was part of Christmas.

'Dress optional,' mused Glyn's father. 'Does that mean my dark suit will do, Nell?'

He called his wife Nell, although no-one could say why, himself included, as her name was Nesta. When asked about it, he would change the subject. He'd been unusually gentle with her since Nain's death, Glyn had noticed, dropping his customary banter and teasing.

When the invitation came, his mother had at first said she wouldn't go. It had just been Nain's funeral, after all, and the party was now just days away. But they'd had a knees-up right after the funeral, Glyn had pointed out. That was family, his mother said. And friends and neighbours, said Glyn. But as the afternoon wore on, she relented, and started talking as if she would be going.

'Suppose it would be rude not to. But you'll need a new tie and a haircut,' she said to her husband.

'Glyn here can give me a going over with the sheep shears, cunna thee, boy?' He winked at Glyn.

His mother got up. 'You take these to the dairy, Alun. I'll go and stick a couple more.'

Alun picked up two freshly-plucked turkeys, which Glyn always thought looked vaguely obscene, and carried them off by their legs.

'What thee grinning at?' his father asked Glyn.

'Did I ever tell you about the time when you and Mam went off for the day somewhere one Sunday and left us to catch a chicken for dinner? Well, we eventually caught it but none of us could stick it like Mam does, not even Alun.'

His mother killed poultry by picking the bird up by its legs, sticking a carving knife in its beak and cutting its wind pipe, all in one smooth, professional movement. She'd hold it there for a couple of minutes, the bird dripping blood, sometimes gently flapping its wings. She held that this was a humane way of slaughter.

'Tom was holding it by the legs and Alun kept making little slashing actions with the carving knife, but he couldn't do it. In the end we took it to the anvil in the Wain House and chopped its head off with the billhook. It kept flapping its wings for ages after. Then we knew what they mean by a headless chicken.'

His father gave one of his body-shaking, wheezing, almost silent laughs.

'So what they going to be cooking up for this do at Glanharan, then?'

'I dunno, all kinds of fancy stuff. Are you looking forward to it?'

'Oh, ah. Don't mind a bit of a do now and again. P'raps you wouldn't think it to look at me now, but I was a bit of a goer in my time.'

Glyn was surprised his father knew what a goer was.

'Bet they'll have all sorts there, people down from London and every-thing.

'Well, thee'll have no trouble fitting in.'

'What do you mean?'

'Oh, I dunno. Thee was always interested in people, different kinds of people. I always said to thee mother thee'd run off with a black woman one day.'

Glyn could see that his father didn't mean this to be a negative. He also used to say Glyn had a bit of the gypsy in him, meaning he didn't want to stay put too long. His father had quite a liking for the gypsies who used to come round the farms in picture-book wooden caravans when he was a boy. They taught him how to bake hedgehogs by wrapping the prickles in clay and putting it in a fire. When it was done you could crack it open like a coconut. Glyn always imagined the scene of his father as a boy sitting with gypsies round their camp fire below the bottom shed, cracking open hedgehogs. When there was a column of mist swirling up on a rise in the wood in early morning, his father would call it Gypsies in the Wood. In his own boyhood Glyn had wished the gypsies would come, so he could have baked hedgehog, but they never did.

He loved his father's stories of old times - how they used to bury carrots in the orchard in what was called a tump, to keep them through the winter. How they would make cider from apples stored in wooden trays in the cel-lar. To this day his father didn't classify cider as alcoholic, and at Christ-mas as a boy he could drink it to his heart's content, as his niece and nephew did now. Apples were still kept in wooden trays in the cellar, but apart from the few his Nain had used to make tarts, most went to rot and had to be thrown away in the spring.

Glyn thought now would be a good time to tell his father about his decision to go to university. He'd thought about it long and hard. Sian was more and more on his mind, but he'd come to the conclusion there was nothing he could do about it. The best thing was for him to leave. His family had a great respect for education, although no-one had ever gone beyond high school. The South Wales cousins especially saw it as a way to keep their sons out of the pit, and a couple had gone down to Cardiff. His father exhibited a rather benign if puzzled tolerance of Glyn's love of books, as he would have put it. Glyn remembered the spring before he had been on the back of the seed drill with his father on the tractor. His job consisted merely of raising the lever as they turned at the end of the field, to pick up the drilling spouts from the ground. It was a perfect time to revise for his mock A levels, with no distractions.

'What thee reading now?' shouted his father back at him over the noise of the engine.

'It's Latin, Dad,' shouted Glyn.

'It's what?'

'Latin,' he shouted louder.

'Latin? Who speaks that then?'

'No-one,' said Glyn. 'It's a dead language.'

'Funny boy,' was all his father said, or shouted, shaking his head with a smile.

Glyn knew that Alun and Tom were in favour of his going. In their gruff, unspoken way they were proud of him. The farm was becoming more and more mechanised, making less work for extra hands. It didn't bring in the money it once did. It wouldn't give him a living, and would mean less for his brothers. His mother he knew wanted him to go and stay in equal measure: it was a kind of battle within her, but in the end it was her ambition for him that was the stronger. Maybe because her own could never have been fulfilled. In her time she had been a gifted and assiduous pupil, but had to leave school at fourteen because she was wanted to work on the her family's farm.

'Oh well, you know your own know-best,' said his father when he told him. 'All good luck to thee. We can manage between us. But remember there's always a home for thee here. And work.'

His mother came in bearing a freshly-stuck turkey.

'Well, the boy's off.'

'Off where?' asked his mother, putting down the turkey with more deliberation than was necessary, as if to delay the moment she had been waiting for and dreading. She knew what was coming.

'I've decided to go to university next year,' said Glyn, concentrating on a burst of particularly energetic feathering.

'Oh well, you know your own know-best,' she said, and the look on her face was inscrutable.

'I love it how you people are so close to your food.'

They all looked to see Luke leaning against the doorpost, cigarette in hand.

'Hmm, maybe too close sometimes,' said Glyn, beginning to feather one of the less pleasant parts of the turkey. He remembered when he was nine or ten, it was already his job to feed the dozen or so cade, or orphan, lambs they kept in the barn after lambing each year. He never thought much of it, until he took a special shine to one lamb which he called Charlie. It was wrong to get sentimental over an animal on a farm. One Sunday dinner his father asked if he was enjoying the lamb.

116

'Thee knows who it is, dussn't thee?' asked his father, who was a great practical joker. Two or three years before they'd all driven to town on market day in the old Morris Oxford as usual. They'd picked up his grandfather and uncle, so it was quite a car full, and Glyn and Tom used to like to ride in the boot with Cymro. When they got into town his father pretended the boot was stuck and they'd have to stay there. They heard the footsteps fade away. It was great fun at first, waiting for his father to come back. But his father waited just long enough for them to think it wasn't a joke after all.

So he wouldn't believe it at first about the lamb.

'It's not. It's not Charlie, is it?' he appealed to his mother. With an apologetic nod she confirmed that it was. He was very upset and, of course, couldn't finish his dinner. When he told this story later in life a particularly concerned social worker asked him if he had got counselling.

'When you've finished with those birds there,' said Luke, 'why don't we go down to the Mucky Duck and see if we can find you a real one,' and winked at Glyn's father.

His father joined in the banter.

'We've got enough mucky ducks here,' he said.

Luke seemed more like his old self that evening. Neither of them referred to the fact that there'd been any kind of distance, or cooling off between them. And Glyn asked the question he'd been wanting to ask for a while.

'So, is the engagement going ahead then?'

'It certainly is,' said Luke. 'But not a word to Ma. It's going to be a big surprise.'

'Well, congratulations. Was Sian surprised when you asked her?'

'In a way. In fact it took a while to bring the old girl around. She said like you, that I was too young and needed to sort myself out a bit first. But I wouldn't take no for an answer. I said we needn't rush into marriage. I don't want her to get away, Glyn. I'm determined to go through with it, no matter what anyone says.'

There didn't seem to be anything more to say on the matter. So Glyn told him of his decision to go to university next year. The two sat in silence for a minute or two. Maybe they both realised that some kind of era, however brief, was about to come to an end.

10

The days left till Christmas flew by in a flurry of feathers and snowflakes. At the farm, it was a family time. His mother ran the kitchen like an army mess, glad no doubt to be able to busy herself and not dwell on her mother's death, on Glyn's decision to leave. Perhaps it had been bad timing on his part to tell them when he did.

Everyone was expected to play his part; to stand around was to invite a new chore. The turkey was the biggest they had ever had, a source of pride even though it would last days after the three households had been through it and had a sickener of it. On Christmas day drinks began at about eleven o'clock with a whisky or sherry, with the men leaving their work to come into the kitchen. It kept flowing all day, unusually for Bryngwanwyn, where there were strict drinking hours.

It was a crisp, clear, bitterly cold day with snow capping the highest hills around. In the kitchen two tables were put end to end and covered with starched white linen cloths. There were twelve for dinner, including Glyn's Auntie Blod and Uncle Ted. It was a home grown dinner, and even though the turkey was such a giant it was juicy, tender and tasty. Two plum puddings which his Nain had made weeks before were brought out burning with brandy and decked with holly, and the children dug for the silver sixpences. The others all raised a glass to Nain, and Glyn could see his mother struggling to eat the pudding.

After dinner and the Queen's speech the tablecloths were removed and whist was played on the green baize cloth underneath, with whisky tumblers and a large glass bowl of nuts. Tom's girlfriend Anwen was a particularly good player and boasted she had won most of their Christmas fare that year at whist drives. Supper was cold turkey and a boiled ham, pickles, beetroot and a potato salad. Then the cards came out again.

With all the festivities and the farm work going on more or less as usual, Glyn didn't give much of a thought to Glanharan. He knew there were people down from London, and Sian was there with Luke, so he left them to their own devices, comfortable here where he belonged. No doubt party preparations were in full swing, and midweek Glyn thought about strolling down there to see if he could lend a hand, but decided against it. He'd probably be more hindrance than help, not really knowing what was what or where to put it. He was, despite himself, excited about the party, but there was an undercoat of nervousness too.

He was half expecting a call from Luke before the big day but it didn't come. So when he set off with his parents just before eight on New Year's Eve he felt something of an interloper, as if he shouldn't really be going with them. His father had scrubbed up well and his mother was elegant but pinch-lipped, giving Glyn funny looks.

'Will I do?' she asked him, as she always did when she was dressed up a bit.

She was wearing a tweedy coat over her smart frock, her mother's butterfly broach pinned to the lapel, and a small hat, a rather drab one thought Glyn, perched on her head. She looked every inch a farmer's wife, and he knew he had no right to wish that she looked anything else.

'You'll do,' he said.

She must have noticed some kind of look on his face, or something in his behaviour.

'You're not worried that we'll show you up, are you?' she asked Glyn as he helped her into the front seat of the Land Rover.

'No, I'm worried that they'll show themselves up,' he said. In reality his concern was about how everyone would get on together. He was nervous, too, about seeing Sian again.

There was a light dusting of snow on the ground which somehow lent the evening an extra touch of expectancy. The drive near the house was already lined with cars and Land Rovers. Glyn wondered if he should drop his parents off at the front door and find somewhere to park but he didn't want them to go in without him. He chanced it and squeezed the vehicle in not far from the house, overshooting the drive a little and occupying a patch of lawn where no-one else had dared.

They climbed out, adjusting their glad rags. Glyn brushed off a bit of straw that had got onto his father's suit. On the front step they met the couple from a nearby farm, their eldest son and his girlfriend. The woman had a drooping mouth, ready to disapprove. Glyn's heart sank a little further. They looked slightly nonplussed at finding themselves in such an unfamiliar situation, not knowing the protocol of what to say. So they made do with some curt How Dos and slightly raised eyebrows as if to say 'God knows what we're doing here.'

It was the first time Glyn had been through the front door and once again he had the vague feeling of being somehow on the wrong side, and felt badly for feeling it. He was conscious of the need to take charge of his family, and now the neighbours, as if they'd be lost without him in this uncharted territory. The door was opened by a stony-faced butler, and Glyn's worst fears were confirmed. Nia had gone for a Hollywood style bash with no holds barred.

As they stepped into the hall though his anxiety and self-consciousness began to disappear. They all stood a moment on the threshold to take in the scene. A fifteen-piece jazz band was playing on the black and white tiles of the huge hall, lined up in tuxedos behind white music stands highlighted with a geometrical motif in silver. Behind them were potted palms. The swinging saxophones and trombones flashed in the lights of the chandelier. Beyond, in the dining room, a heavily-laden long white table with pleated full-length cloths bore all kinds of picture-perfect food and next to it there was a fully-fledged bar with gleaming punch bowls and champagne in silver ice buckets. Waitresses in black handed round silver salvers of hors d'oeuvres. Bouquets and garlands of white lilies were the finishing touch.

Glyn glanced at his companions and was relieved to see that they were as taken as he was, except for the disapproving neighbour whose mouth drooped further into a grimace. And his mother was frowning at the floral arrangements. She disapproved of cut flowers in the house but seemed to be viewing these with particular scorn.

'She shouldn't bring lilies inside,' she said in a warlike whisper to Glyn. 'It means a death in the house.'

'Shush, Mam!' said Glyn, and noticed her face soften. He followed her gaze and saw Nia was approaching them. He could only hope she hadn't heard. She was wearing a long, silver, satin, off-the-shoulder dress and seemed more serene, and sober, than Glyn had seen her for a long time. She welcomed the party with the utmost grace that put them at their ease, ordering drinks and waving them towards the food at the same time. His mother, too, was gracious, if a little cold. Seamlessly, Nia took Glyn by the arm and led him away from the others.

'Luke isn't here yet. He's picking up Sian.' Glyn had always been struck by the way Nia would know what you wanted to know without having to ask it. 'They should be here any minute.'

'You're looking really.....stunning,' said Glyn. He wished he could have found a more sophisticated way of saying it.

'Why, thank you, kind Sir.' She gave a mock curtsey and his cheek a peck. 'Oops, excuse me, I'll have to behave myself in front of your Ma, won't I now?'

She had clearly made an effort to stay sober, was playing the part of the hostess to perfection and seemed to relish the role.

Glyn threaded his way through the buzzing crowd, nodding as he went, and joined his parents at the bar. Like almost everyone else, they seemed surprisingly relaxed, taking it in their stride. Again, he had been worrying over nothing. His father had already sunk the better part of a pint. His mother had allowed herself a glass of champagne. Stockton was circulating making sure that glasses were filled and charming people with his seasoned, insincere bonhomie. Even Briddy looked serene and sublime in copper velvet and most people quickly warmed to her soft-spoken charm.

'She's pulled it off,' thought Glyn as he surveyed the glittering gathering.

The door flew open and Luke and Sian stumbled in on a gust of wind, stomping snow from their shoes. The band finished a familiar Glen Miller wartime number and the buzz of the room died away as everyone turned to admire the golden couple. Sian looked glamorous in a long red dress, her hair piled up on top of her head. Glyn could barely take his eyes off her. Luke by contrast was dashingly scruffy in a blue velvet jacket and an open-necked frilly shirt falling out of his jeans. Glyn was never quite sure whether this casual chic came naturally to him or if it was crafted effortlessness. But there was no doubt about it, they made a striking pair.

The age difference was not really discernible. Glyn didn't know whether this was because Sian looked young or Luke looked older than his years. Probably a bit of both.

Nia went to greet them, and there was no mistaking the look of pride on her face. She hugged Sian, took Luke by the elbow and guided him down the steps towards the bar. On the way the couple greeted Glyn's party warmly and his parents in turn responded cordially, still a little awkward and stiff when it came to making small talk. Nia stood behind them, and all of a sudden Glyn caught a strange, strained look upon her face. He wondered why. Things seemed to be going so well. People were getting on. Some of his anxieties returned. He looked at his mother. She was clearly charmed by the couple. It was what he had been hoping for, wasn't it? The people he loved most, his two worlds, were in harmony at last. Yet his eyes kept straying to Nia. He was struck by the unfamiliar pinched mouth, knotted brow, white face. Wasn't the evening a huge success for her? What she'd wanted, yearned for? Everyone being together, admiring her golden couple, having a damn good time. What did she have to worry about?

Luke excused himself and Sian and took her to be introduced to more guests. Nia seemed lost in a world of her own, but had enough presence of mind to follow them and help with the introductions. Glyn's current of unease continued and he couldn't quite put his finger on the source. He should be enjoying himself at last, relaxing now that things were going so well after so much worry. But he kept looking out for Nia, trying to see how she was, puzzling about what had come over her.

After a few introductions she disappeared with Luke, in the direction of the study, and they left Sian with Briddy. Glyn caught Sian's eye. She smiled at him, but he could see straightway that she too was distracted by something, worried, even as she charmed all around her with her easy conversation. In a few minutes Glyn caught her eye again – she seemed to be seeking his out too – and he tried to give her a subtle look which asked, 'Everything's alright, isn't it?'

Her eyes replied, 'I hope so. I don't know. Let's try to have a good time.'

Nia and Luke reappeared. Clearly there had been words of some sort. They were flushed – unlike them both. Nia was now too forced in her bonhomie, overplaying her role of hostess. Luke was at Sian's side, an arm around her waist. Beneath his smile he looked angry, and there was something else. What was it?

Glyn's eyes met Sian's again.

'Are things better now?'

'I don't think so,' came the silent reply. 'I don't know what's going on.'

Glyn looked around. The party was in full swing. No-one else seemed to sense there was anything remotely out of the ordinary. Stockton and Briddy were busy doing the rounds, keeping the flow of food and wine going, keeping guests happy. His parents, he was surprised to see, were now mingling even with complete strangers, exotic creatures from the London set, looking as if they'd been going to parties like this all their lives. It was just the four of them, him, Nia, Luke and Sian who knew that something was going on behind the scenes.

Glyn lost sight of Luke and Sian for quite a while. He circulated through the rooms, stopping to talk to friends, but keeping an eye out for the couple. He bumped into Piers and Laura, who seemed to be the only friends of Luke to have come down from London. They seemed a little lost themselves, and pleased to see him.

'Have you seen that old bastard Luke anywhere?' asked Piers.

'Not for a while, no,' said Glyn.

'So this is where you hide out?' said Laura. 'I had no idea that Wales was so swinging.'

'Oh, yes,' said Glyn, looking around him. 'This is pretty standard.'

'No kidding?' said Laura, opening her eyes wide.

'Yes, kidding.'

Laura smiled. He liked her. She was a strange mix of suave and gauche, of cool and goofy. He maybe recognised something of himself in her. He suspected that, like him, she was still looking for her way in life, for where she wanted to be. He wondered if, deep down, she was lonely. In an odd kind of way, she boosted his confidence. He could almost feel it growing, even as his friends at Glanharan seemed, for whatever reason, to be losing their poise.

They soon ran out of things to say, and Glyn tore himself away and went over to chat to Johnny Jones. As he did, he caught sight of Nia just standing there by the window, as if not quite knowing where she was. He wanted to go up and talk to her, but it would be rude to tear himself away from Johnny Jones just yet.

Eventually he did get away and went up to her. A little group was around her, talking at her. She was speaking her lines, but her mind was clearly elsewhere.

He cupped her elbow with his hand.

'Can I get you a drink, Nia?' he asked in a low voice. He'd noticed that, almost incredibly, she had no glass in her hand.

'What?' she said with a frown, not quite looking at him.

'Can I get you a drink?' he said.

'No. No, thank you, I'm fine.'

'Are you alright?'

'I'm fine, I tell you.' It was almost a snarl. It was the first time she'd been anything less than gracious to him.

The band blared on and played more upbeat numbers from the 'Forties and 'Fifties as well as recent hits. So there were tunes that everyone recognised, and the hall was now full of dancers – twisters, jivers, even waltzers. It was clearly a great party for everyone else. His father was at the bar, having a whale of a time with his cronies. Dolly, a distant cousin of his mother who'd started cleaning for Nia at Glanharan, milled around talking to people as if she went to parties like this every week. Even the woman with the disapproving mouth was finding lots to wag her chin about with a group of wives sitting on chairs lining the walls. His mother was close by with another group. She beckoned Glyn over with her finger.

'Your father's getting a bit tight,' she said. 'You'd better take us home. You don't want him making a fool of himself.'

It was only half an hour to go before midnight, before the New Year, the new decade even, and part of Glyn didn't want to leave. Not only did he think they should see the New Year in, but he wanted to find out what was going on. On the other hand, part of him would be relieved to go. He didn't want to see Nia, Luke and Sian have to sing Auld Lang Syne, pretending to be enjoying themselves, pretending everything was alright when it so clearly wasn't. And his father was indeed getting into quite a state. There was nothing for it but to say his goodbyes.

He found Luke sitting in a leather chair by the fire, flushed with the heat and the brandy. He seemed pensive now, preoccupied. He looked up and gave Glyn a weak, lopsided smile.

'Oh, there you are.'

Glyn just about made out the words, they were so slurred.

'Where's Sian?' asked Glyn.

'Dunno. Talking to some old codgers. They fly to her like moths to a flame'

'Is there anything wrong?'

'Wrong. What could possibly be wrong?'

There was bitterness in his voice.

'Aren't you going to make your announcement?'

Luke was staring into the flames. He seemed no longer to be concentrating on what Glyn was saying.

'I've got to go now, take my family home. My father's a bit the worse for wear.'

He looked up at Glyn again, and smiled as if he were seeing him for the first time again.

'Who isn't?' said Luke. 'You can't possibly go now. We have to say goodbye to the Sixties.'

'I'm sorry, I have to,' said Glyn.

'Goodbye Sixties,' shouted Luke, flinging out his arms and spilling the contents of his brandy glass, 'and good riddance.'

'Well, say goodbye to Sian for me.'

Luke suddenly grabbed Glyn by the arm and pulled him close. Glyn could smell his boozy breath.

'Glyn. Glyn.'

'What?'

'Glyn. Come down tomorrow morning. It's very important. We can have a hair of the dog.'

'Well......'

'Glyn. Promise me. It's important. Promise.'

Glyn promised.

11

Glyn didn't wake till about eleven. When they'd got back to the farm the night before, his father had insisted on them seeing the New Year in with a glass. He and Glyn had drunk whisky, his Mother had sherry. He wished now he hadn't. It was an effort to get out of bed, especially as it was so cold, with a film of frost lining the inside of his bedroom window. As he was washing, he remembered the strange behaviour at the party last night, and then his promise to Luke to go down to Glanharan that morning. He wouldn't bother, he decided. It was already too late, and the last thing he wanted was a hair of the dog.

Yet the more he thought about it, and he couldn't help thinking about it, the more he wanted to get to the bottom of the mystery. And he *had* promised......

So after dinner he found himself jumping into the Land Rover and making his way carefully down the frosty and empty roads to Glanharan. He found them all in the kitchen, drinking coffee and eating toast, looking as if they'd just got up. Some were having Buck's Fizz and bits and pieces of leftovers from the party. He and Sian exchanged quick glances, and hers suggested that she was still none the wiser about what the problem was last night. Luke seemed pleased to see him, but he was subdued. Nia alone seemed to have recovered some of her composure, as if nothing had happened, although she was not joining her friends in the champagne. Glyn felt more than ever that she was playing a part, and not totally convincingly.

There were a few people Glyn didn't know, houseguests from London. There was no sign of Piers or Laura. The others were swapping stories about the party and had clearly found the locals very entertaining. It was as if they were commenting on strange animals in a zoo

'And did you see that man in the flat cap trying to do the Charleston....?'

Nia told them to stop. She hated post-mortems, she said, and got bored by stories of who did what. The houseguests looked confused, as if this was news to them, and exchanged puzzled grins.

'I think we all need a good walk to blow away the cobwebs,' said Nia.

Luke looked appalled, and so did the houseguests. Glyn had never before heard her suggest exercise of any kind. But she seemed to have made up her mind. She suggested a walk on Bryn Grwnan, the bleak ridge across the valley, named after the way the wind howled mournfully through the rocks. It was popular with hikers, rambling groups and so on who came from miles away, but the locals wondered what on earth they could see in it and stayed well clear.

Nia commandeered Glyn to take them in the Land Rover as far as the road went.

'The London lot won't want to come,' she said, waving a dismissive arm in their direction. 'No stamina.'

The London lot looked hugely relieved.

Sian said nothing, her eyes on Luke. No-one moved. But Luke seemed to be warming to the idea.

'Maybe a walk would do us good,' he said, looking at Sian.

'Come on, Briddy,' said Nia, knowing who to tackle first. 'Get them moving.'

Briddy got slowly up from her chair, clearly puzzled herself by Nia's sudden enthusiasm, and Luke and Sian did the same. Nia had disappeared upstairs and came down more or less pushing Stockton in front of her. She helped him and the others get kitted out in jumpers, coats, boots, gloves and woolly hats.

It was a nasty day, foggy and freezing at the same time, with forlorn patches of snow on the lawn. It would be even worse on the mountain. Glyn couldn't see why she wanted to go today of all days, but there was obviously no denying her now.

And so they set out, Glyn, Nia and Sian on the front bench of the Land Rover, the rest huddled under rugs in the back. No-one said very much. Glyn drove up to the old quarry, as far as the lane went, and they piled out miserably. It was a daunting sight, the steep ascent in such conditions, but Nia started walking. They trooped up behind her without a word. Glyn found his heart sinking. He'd thought Nia would have got bored by the time they got here, but on the contrary she seemed to have a missionary zeal about the expedition. What earthly good could come of this? A little fresh air, all well and good, but it was getting foggier and icier as they climbed, the fog and snow producing an eerie, almost noisy silence. Surely this was getting a little dangerous? He really didn't think it was a good idea.

He could see the others having the same thoughts, glancing nervously at each other, then ahead at Nia, head down, plodding determinedly on. They filed on behind her, bowing their heads against the cold, concentrating on their footing.

'What you do in the name of friendship,' muttered Briddy to Glyn. She seemed close to mutiny.

'Don't worry, I know this place like the back of my hand,' shouted Nia.

'How could she possibly?' thought Glyn. 'She might know the region and the terrain, but she doesn't know the ridge. Hardly anyone does.'

He kept telling himself he should take command, warn people back. He knew inwardly that's what was required, yet he couldn't. He wondered why Luke didn't, clearly against the thing at the start. He glanced back at him. He looked grim, determined. Maybe he didn't want to lose face to his mother. Nia's spirit was stronger.

They fumbled their way towards the ridge. Glyn knew how narrow people said it was, how steep the slopes either side. He kept telling himself, 'Put a stop to it now. It's madness in this fog.'

Why didn't he? Why couldn't he?

Nia soldiered relentlessly on. Without a word, the others started arming each other; Luke and Sian, Glyn and Briddy. Stockton walked on ahead and tried to do the same to Nia, but she shrugged him off, striding ahead with a dogged determination that Glyn had never seen in her before. She seemed to have a purpose. He couldn't begin to guess what it was.

As they reached the ridge itself, Nia seemed to lose a little steam and slowed down somewhat. Luke strode up towards her, as if to take the baton, as if it was a battle of wills between them. Stockton was now lagging behind them, and the other three brought up the rear. The path across the ridge, a sheep's path, was narrow, with room for only one at a time. The file of reluctant walkers trudged on in silence, watching their footing. It was eerily quiet – no humming, no wind howling through the crags.

All of a sudden there was a scream, an unnatural scream, more of a bestial yowl. Glyn peered forward into the fog and walked a little faster, followed by Sian and Briddy. He could just about make out Stockton, half crawling over to where the scream came from.

He shouted back to the others, 'She's fallen over the edge.'

They made their way to the sound of his voice as quickly as they dared, half crawling as he had, clawing the rocks with their hands. Despite the fog, Glyn could sense the edge of the ridge. As he made out the fall of the land below them, he could just about discern Nia's head below them. She was clinging to a bush on the steep slope with both hands, uttering not a sound, but looking up at them with an awful, pleading look on her face. She wasn't that far below them. She was just within reach. Glyn heard Briddy give a kind of strangled screech.

'Just hold on, Nia,' shouted Stockton. 'We can reach you. I'll come down to get you.'

'No, Stockton,' said Luke, resolute and masterful as Glyn had never seen him. 'I'll do it. I'm younger and stronger than you. And taller. If you and Glyn hold my legs I can reach her.'

Stockton hesitated for just a second, looking for some reason back up at Briddy. She nodded, and in doing so took charge of the situation. Glyn and Stockton looked at each other and Luke was already lying flat on the ridge.

They each took a leg and lowered him down inch by inch, hand over hand, until they had him by the shins.

'Let me lower,' he shouted. 'Lower, lower. I can't quite reach her. I'm almost there. Ma, give me one hand. You can do it. You'll be OK. I'm almost there.'

They could see the terrified Nia slowly let go of the bush with one hand, and stretch it towards the hand of her son. They seemed within reach, their hands touching, but still Luke didn't grab it.

'More, more,' he shouted back up at them. 'I'm almost there. I'm OK, I'm OK.'

Glyn and Stockton looked at each other. Their hands and arms were aching already. Could they hold him by the feet? Could they pull them both back up?

They looked down. Nia's body was flat against the rock. She could hardly speak. But her face was eloquent enough.

'Do it, do it,' she croaked. 'Whatever he says, do it.'

Glyn closed his eyes with the strain of holding him just below the ankles. Surely he could get hold of her now?

He opened them just in time to see Nia grab at Luke's forearm with a jerk. And before he knew what was happening Luke's feet slid through their hands, he flipped heels over head, and with breath-wrenching yelps somersaulted to his death down the mountainside.

Part Two

12

Yes, it's me, Glyn. You've been wanting me to tell the whole story – beginning, middle and end – spanning some thirty-five years. I won't spare you any details, as terrible as they sometimes are, because I know that wouldn't do. Too much has been kept secret for too long, and as we know, secrets are never good. There's always a price to pay in the end. It seems right to start writing as me now as I try to answer some unanswered questions for you, Sian. On with the story.

That photo I found in the attic in Glanharan ten years ago now brought it all back so clearly, so instantly, that it must have all been somewhere not too deep in my mind. Only some of the details were misty. In that intervening quarter of a century I'd thought about them a great deal, going over it all again and again. It was a haunting experience to see you all lined up higgedly-piggedly in the back yard, your funny clothes and haircuts giving you an innocent air, certainly innocent of what was to come.

It's said that the past is another country, but one to which we cannot travel. It's another dimension. It was hard for me to accept that those days and what happened since were in the same place, one continuum. The tragedy on Bryn Grwnan ended a certain episode in my life, a fascinating interlude. I hadn't seen any of the people involved since. Except one, of course. You.

After the inquest on Luke returned a verdict of accidental death, Nia shut Glanharan up and moved away. It was boarded up for three years, no For Sale signs to be seen. On visits back to Bryngwanwyn I would wander down there sometimes on a fine day, and each time see a few more signs of decay: a slipped tile here, a broken window pane there, until it was almost back in the same condition as before, ivy and grass reclaiming every lovingly-tended corner.

Then it was bought by the county social services department and turned into some kind of home for adolescent boys in trouble. It became a kind of no-go place. When I found the photo, the house had just been turned into flats. We'd bought one, you and I - somewhere to come back to for long weekends and holidays. We needed somewhere to stay. When they retired, Mam and Dad had built a small bungalow at the bottom of Bryngwanwyn lane where the milkstand used to be, and Alun and his family had moved into the house. We couldn't impose on them all the time.

When we started looking for a small flat, the ones at Glanharan had just come on to the market and there weren't many others nearby. I had misgivings at first – something to do with unearthing the past. But you – a little strangely I thought – were enthusiastic. When we went to see it, my doubts subsided. The flat we liked best was on the top floor, facing into the woods with no views of Bryn Grwnan. The bedroom where I used to stay had been turned into two small ones. The décor was strictly neutral: magnolia walls and wooden floors. It was a different place from the one Nia had created.

The attic above our flat hadn't been touched. It was only when I was putting in some shelving, trying to turn it into a useful storage space, that I found the photo, sticking out from under a beam. God knows what it was doing there. It's amazing how you can find things in the strangest of places and wonder about the precise moment they were dropped or put there.

It was natural I suppose, looking back, that after Luke's death you and I should console each other. We sought each other out, going for quiet drinks in pubs we'd never been to before, taking long walks on well-trodden paths.

For a long time we did not have much to say, or rather did not know how to put it into words. So we muttered the inane ones that come readily to hand at times like this, not nearly adequate enough to bridge the space between us, the space still occupied by Luke, preventing intimacy. Yet we understood things without having to say much, and fell into a rhythm of needing each other.

One thing we did talk about was the strange goings-on the night before the tragedy. You were at as much of a loss as I was to explain them. You told me that Luke had been in the best of moods that night, before they got to the party. You told me you'd had your doubts about the engagement at first, which I have to confess now I was pleased to hear, but Luke had won you round. He could be so persuasive. He said it could just be a bit of fun. He was so looking forward to the big announcement, to the surprise on everyone's face. But before he had a chance to say anything, Nia started acting strangely. She and Luke went for a long talk in the study. He came back looking like thunder, in a foul mood. He wouldn't tell you what had been said, brushed it off, said it was something he'd forgotten to do for his mother. You knew there was more to it than that. But he'd get even more furious when she asked him about it.

I told you I'd noticed something between the three of them. You asked me what it could be. I had no idea. I'd turned it over and over in my mind enough times since then, but couldn't come up with anything. What could possibly have happened to change things in an instant, to transform Nia from a happy hostess, enjoying the party she'd spent so long planning, into someone who seemed to have the cares of the world on her shoulder? You felt the same. It wasn't as if Luke had announced the engagement. He'd been in such a filthy mood that he never did. He made some flimsy excuse about waiting until Nia was in a better mood. So it wasn't even that that could have upset her. Mothers could be funny about letting their sons go to another woman, you said, but Nia had always been so fond of you. Now you had also lost touch with her. No-one seemed to know where she was. So you'd never been able to ask her what had gone wrong.

The autumn after Luke's death I went away to university in Aberystwyth to study English. I came home most weekends in a battered old Mini van which had its bonnet tied down by a piece of red flex. We called it The Shed, you and I, for I saw you most weekends, and despite the age difference we became a couple. It seemed so natural, and I knew, had known for a while, that you were the one for me. I remembered Luke saying the same when I questioned him about the age difference between him and you.

After graduating I got a job as a reporter on the Welsh Mail in Cardiff. You came to live with me, and found a teaching job easily enough. Of course we didn't forget about Luke, but he was with us now, not between us. We thought about Nia too, and from time to time I made half-hearted attempts to reach her. You were curious about what had happened to her, but didn't seem to want to pursue it in any way. I'd barely talked to her after that day on Bryn Grwnan. I tried to visit of course but she was hardly in a fit state in those first few days and even when I did see her for a few moments at the funeral there were so few words to say. I think you went to see her too, but it was a brief, unsatisfactory meeting. Nia was too upset to talk much.

Everyone from miles around seemed to come to Luke's funeral. Even though he had breezed into their lives so briefly he seemed to have made his mark, and people were overcome with sympathy for Nia, shaking their heads and closing their eyes when the tragedy inevitably came up in conversation. Even Mam immediately forgot her past reservations and insisted on a large wreath, sent food down with me to Glanharan as was the custom, and wrote a long letter to Nia which she wouldn't let me see.

The day of the funeral was a freezing, still January day and Nia was half-carried into the overflowing little chapel by Stockton and Briddy. Her face was drained of blood and her body almost of life: she seemed a broken woman, hardly realising where she was. For once she didn't seem as if she was playing a part. Scruffy wisps of hair blew from under a simple headscarf, her paleness unmasked by make-up.

At the inquest she mumbled and stumbled through her testimony. All she could remember was hanging on to the bush. She could barely look up, her face hugging the rock, was only dimly aware of the commotion above. Then she could just about make out Luke's wild face from the corner of her eye, heard shouts, saw his hand come closer, closer, felt it grab hold of her, felt its warmth for an instant before it was gone again, gone for ever.

Everything after that was hazy. She must have found a foothold on the rock, inched herself up until she caught Stockton's hand and was hauled to safety.

After she left little was heard of her for a long while. Word was she had gone back to America. After two or three years she began to make the odd appearance in American soaps or TV movies, small character parts that were probably needed to eke out a living: maverick aunts, eccentric piano teachers, feisty landladies. I think I wrote to one of the TV networks asking for her contact details but heard nothing back. This was, of course, in the days before Google.

It was hard to judge from these appearances much about her own, or how she was bearing up, as they seemed to call for heavy make-up. There was little press coverage that I saw, a paragraph here and there and if there was a little single-column picture it was from the pre-Glanharan days, one of her old glamour shots. I'd read more about Stockton who'd gone on to make quite a name for himself in Hollywood with two or three box-office hits under his belt. It seemed he and Nia had split up soon after she left Wales.

I thought about her often and when I did a rather hackneyed image of the faded, lonely star came into my head. She would be sitting in a small, shabby apartment, or more probably hotel room, in Manhattan, listening to a scratchy record of Ella Fitzgerald, looking at old photographs, a glass of vodka tilted slightly in her hand. Perhaps a kindly neighbour who did some shopping for her now and then had called, and was guardedly asking about some old Hollywood great.

'Ah, dear old darling Jimmy', Nia would sigh, casting her eyes skywards and drifting off into her own memories, a wistful smile playing on her somewhat distorted lips. Then she would notice her glass was emptier than she would like and demand a refill. Nia never had spoken about Holly-wood very much, even when you asked her about the stars. Sometimes I would wonder how well she knew anybody. But then she'd notice an obit in the paper, or catch an old black and white film on TV, and she'd drop a throwaway comment: 'He could never suffer in silence - in fact he needed a loud-hailer and a captive audience' or 'She was another one with a wel-come mat outside her bedroom door'. Wherever she was, would she be giving a thought for her days at Glanharan? Or would she have banished such thoughts, blotted it all out?

These memories and speculations were accompanied by a niggling guilt that I should have made more of an effort to find her. But as the years passed it seemed more and more remote a possibility, until one day, about a month after I found the photograph, I happened to see that Nia was to appear in the West End, in quite a small role as Diana Rigg's mother in a Tennessee Williams play. It seemed a golden opportunity. My simmering curiosity about what happened the night before Luke's death began to bubble.

I tried to figure out a way of getting to see her, when another co-inci-dence presented itself. I was by now feature writer on a national paper in London. We were in the editorial meeting, planning Christmas coverage. The features editor was proposing a series of interviews - 'with the old stars who still come into our living rooms every Christmas' was how she put it.

I'm not sure I would have gone for it ordinarily. It wasn't a bad idea, not exactly original, but seemed to go down OK with the others in the morning conference. Remember it was still the time when families gathered round their TV sets. We tried out some names.

'What about Nia Barry?' I said.

'God, is she still alive?' said the editor, a crusty old man from the old school. 'She must be knocking on a bit.'

'She'd only be in her early seventies,' I said. People round the table seemed surprised. She belonged to another age.

'She's in the West End with Diana Rigg,' I said. 'And that old standard *A Midnight Clear* is still very popular. I knew her. I could track her down quite easily.'

'Not again,' said the news editor. 'That tragedy in Wales is drummed up year after year. Had a creepy name, that hill. What was it? Howling Hill. Death on Howling Hill,' he said, his face beaming as if he had just solved a riddle.

'Well in fact I looked her up, and it's a good fifteen years since we did anything on her. Nobody else has done much either. And she'll be on the London stage. It's got the Whatever Happened To? factor about it.'

I wasn't quite sure how much to push my own involvement, or how I'd write it if it ever came to it. But that was for another day.

'Could you make something of it?' asked the deputy editor, chewing his glasses and raising a bored eyebrow at me.

'It was a pretty dramatic story at the time. And I was there. It could be quite interesting to see wha....'

'You were there?' asked the editor, clearly implying that I should have spoken up before now.

'She was our neighbour in Wales.'

'You were there when her son went over that hill?'

'I was.'

'So what happened?'

I said I couldn't add much to what was already out there.

'But you were there. What you think, Jo?' he said, turning to the features editor. She was Canadian, a tough old boot whose stock response to a bad idea was, 'Blow it out your ass.'

'Could breathe some new life into it,' she said through a cloud of cigarette smoke and couldn't have sounded more bored.

'OK,' said the editor to me. 'See what you can come up with, but don't spend too much time on it. Or money.'

After conference I followed Jo into her office and we fleshed the idea out.

'Alrighty. Five features with names from top Christmas films,' she said, blowing smoke straight in my face and crushing the cigarette vigorously into a jam doughnut on her desk. She stared at me over the top of her glasses - she wore them on a chain but never took them off or looked through them. All she needed was a monocle and a cigarette holder and she'd be straight out of an Otto Dix painting.

'One week in the States and one week here should do it. Let me know what you can stand up by the end of the week.'

It was only then that I started to think about the implications of what I'd let myself in for, and what you would make of it all. You'd gone quiet the month before when I showed you the photo at Glanharan, and put it down with just a faint smile without saying anything. But I caught you peering at it later when you thought I wasn't looking. I couldn't decipher the look on your face, but it wasn't exactly happy.

When I mentioned the possible interview with Nia you were unusually non-committal, but I got the impression you didn't want me to do it, although you didn't say so in so many words. You just asked if it was wise, and I wasn't quite sure what you meant.

The next day I checked over all the stuff on Nia I'd got out of the cuttings library. The older stories were still pasted onto pages in large red folders. Up till then I hadn't given much thought to Nia's early years, trying to break into show business. Of her childhood in Wales there was barely a mention – she clearly disliked talking about it. So her story, as far as the press was concerned, started when she came to London as a seventeen-year-old ingénue looking for work. She found it as an artist's model in Charlotte Street, posing, if the cuttings were to be believed, for some well-known artists who lived and worked in bohemian Fitzrovia before the war. Between the lines it inferred that she wasn't exactly required to dress for the occasion. When war came, she toured with ENSA and then started getting small parts in the West End until TV started taking off, and she started doing work in the live productions at Alexander Palace.

It was quite a step from the hills of Wales to life in the London media circles, I reflected – one that had taken me years. It would have taken guts, and I wondered what had driven her to take it. I pictured her getting off a steaming train at Euston, carrying a battered suitcase. It made me see her in a different light. I wondered if she'd talk about it in the interview, and found myself becoming more and more intrigued.

I got hold of the press release about the play. I rang the PR company to get her agent's address. It was to open in three weeks and I had to get a move on. No doubt she was already in London for rehearsals.

I got the number from a distinctly unenthusiastic young woman in the PR agency in Soho. Nia's agent was in New York, so I faxed him the details of the series and asking for an interview, when and wherever it was convenient. I got a fax back the next afternoon asking who would do the interview and how long we would want. That was another thing I hadn't given much thought to. If Nia saw my name, would it work for me or against? I didn't have much choice though - she would find out sooner or later, so faxed back again, saying time was of the essence as we needed this for the run up to Christmas.

For the rest of the afternoon I worked at fixing up some of the other interviews, and was quite pleased with the progress, but although I kept glancing over to the fax machine with pleading expressions it stayed obstinately quiet.

Next morning I went straight to the fax before dumping my things at my desk and there were the usual coils of paper, some of it spilling over onto the floor. I gathered them up and rifled through them until I recognised the agent's logo. Miss Barry would like to know the scope of the interview.

She'd taken the bait. Curiosity had got the better of her, I assumed. I felt the kind of thrill I used to get years ago when landing a big interview. Only this wasn't about the interview. It was about seeing Nia again. Past doubts disappeared.

I decided it would be better to ring the agent that afternoon. He was cagier than I expected, asking for a full list of questions in advance, which I resisted of course, as I didn't want to relinquish editorial control. I gave him the range of the interview: career over the last few years, New York lifestyle, feelings about coming back to the UK and so on.

Well, he'd have to consult Miss Barry again. He'd call me back. He did, quite quickly. It would have to be in a restaurant in London - she didn't want anyone going backstage or to her hotel. I suggested The Ivy, which I didn't like very much myself, but thought we could be discrete among the theatrical crowd. And I thought she'd like it. It was very Nia, or used to be. I didn't know what she was like now. We pinned down the time. No, she didn't want picking up, but I was to be punctual, so she wouldn't be alone. I was surprised it had all happened so fast.

In the next few days I nailed the other interviews without too much trouble, one in a flat in Soho around the corner from Stockton's place where I went with Luke all those years ago, one in a cottage in Borehamwood, one in Santa Barbara and one in Sardi's, the theatre restaurant in New York. I'd do the Americans ones first and Nia's last. This way I could knock off all the others and have them ready to go, and so time the piece about Nia so it came out just before opening night.

It all went surprisingly smoothly, producing some interesting material and I found myself enjoying it more than I thought I would. The trick with old stars was to think of ways to stop them being bored, to come up with something fresh. They would have been answering the same questions for years. And on the other end of the scale you avoid coming across as an ignoramus who knew nothing about them. That would just incur their wrath and put them in the driving seat. You had to flatter without fawning, try to engage them in a proper conversation, and not try to be too clever. If they relaxed, lowered their guard, they'd give a far better interview.

So I was especially assiduous in my research, not just relying on the library cuttings which tended to regurgitate the same clichés and mistakes. I got hold of some biographies and autobiographies, and even went to the

World Cinema shop in St Martin's Lane to buy some of their old films that I hadn't seen.

I enjoyed the trip to California and New York. My research paid off and the interviews went well. There was something touching about meeting these old stars as they faced their final curtain, and once they did relax they talked more freely, perhaps no longer feeling the need to put up a front, to give off a predetermined image of themselves. They could look back over their lives with a candour that they must have found refreshing. I got some good stuff, and Jo was pleased.

'I didn't think much of the idea when you mentioned it,' she said when she'd read through some of it. 'Bit hackneyed. But they're a good read.' I didn't point out that the idea had been hers in the first place.

There was only Nia to go, and she of course would be a different kettle of fish. I had no idea what to expect. The night before the meeting I was so nervous and restless I couldn't sleep. You asked what was wrong. I mumbled something fairly trite. Somehow I hadn't told you that I was going through with the interview with Nia, and you hadn't asked. I didn't fully understand why I was being so secretive, and something was making me uneasy.

13

I got to The Ivy in plenty of time at seven twenty and was shown to a table in the corner under the stained-glass windows. I ordered a Jack Daniels to give me Dutch courage - it would be quite a wait if the old Nia was anything to go by. Old. Funny, before now I hadn't really tried to picture how she'd look. The publicity pics the PR people sent out were clearly quite old too, and showed the familiar, glamorous Nia and that's how I thought of her. I hadn't managed to dredge up any more recent.

Then I saw her come through into the lobby, well cut white-blond, straight hair framing her face, dark glasses, a roll-neck black sweater under a camel-hair coat. Nothing too showy, but stylish. Before the Maitre D had time to welcome her she had spotted me after one brisk look around the room. She waved him away and strode assuredly towards me, holding out her hand as she approached the table. But when I stood up and held out mine she put hers on my shoulder and kissed me on both cheeks, then gave me a hug.

'Glyn,' she said softly. 'It's been a long time.'

I was surprised at how much shorter she was than me - I remembered us being about the same height. And her American accent and ways were both more pronounced. But otherwise she was the Nia I knew, looking older of course, but not her years.

'Vodka martini, onion, straight up,' she said to the waiter, 'and another for my young friend here. He's a very distinguished journalist, you know.'

As he took her coat and slid her chair smoothly in under her, she gave me one of her old mischievous grins.

'I'm sorry I didn't have you round to my hotel,' she said, 'but I didn't quite know what to expect'

'Oh please,' I said, and realised this was going to be even trickier than I'd bargained for. Should I catch up on old times, ask the questions I really wanted to ask, or go quickly into interview mode? Or try to combine the two?

Nia spared me the trouble of trying to work these things out, and waded straight in as if we had just bumped into each other after a few months, ignoring the interview part altogether. In fact she started interviewing me.

'Now tell me what you've been doing with yourself since I last saw you. You've done well for yourself, haven't you? I always knew you would.'

It was all I could do to keep myself from staring at her, both because I was seeing her after all these years and because she did look remarkably well. She'd turned into one of those older women who defy age - she seemed indeed to have improved with it.

She appeared delighted to hear all my news, and knew about me and you, although I wasn't clear how, and asked about children.

'One son. Twelve. A good boy.'

'Of course. What's his name?'

This was one thing I had given some thought to, with some dread, but there was nothing to do other than come straight out with it.

'Luke,' I said, with a rather crumpled smile.

She swallowed hard, as if bracing herself for something. To fill the silence I told her about Glanharan and the photo. A cloud passed over her eyes. The waiter came to take our order.

'Maybe you don't want to talk about it,' I said when he'd gone. 'I'm sorry, it was clumsy of me. I shouldn't have mentioned it.'

'Oh Glyn, we can't really avoid it. And of course we shouldn't. I'm delighted that you called your son... Luke, really.' But she couldn't get the name out first off, and had to have a second run at it.

She was looking over my left shoulder, her eyes just a little downcast, her tongue moistening her top lip.

'I did try to get in touch, you know.'

'Yes, I do know. I just couldn't face it for a long time, Glyn. I had to learn to be alone, with apologies to a certain Miss Garbo. You might have read that Stockton and I split up not long afterwards. Grief does that to some couples. A silence takes over. We were never that strong, to be honest. For a while, I lived in London with Briddy, my only real friend. People always assume that if you're in the spotlight you're surrounded by amusing, devoted friends. But it can be the loneliest place in the world. I couldn't have come through it without her. She was the best friend I ever had. But then that wretched Henry's wife eventually died, and Briddy married him. It was what she had been waiting for for years, she who had never had much happiness in her own life. I couldn't deny it her, stand in her way. So I went back to New York, and I didn't see her for a long time. I'm going to look her up while I'm here.'

'I felt bad that we never really talked properly afterwards - you know, after Luke tried to pull you up at Bryn Grwnan,' I said.

She seemed to be making her mind up about something and ordered another vodka martini before the wine arrived.

'He didn't,' she said finally.

'I know he didn't, but he tried, Nia.'

'He didn't,' she said again. 'He didn't try to pull me up. He tried to push me down.'

She was so casual about it that I don't think it registered at first. I must have started to say something else before doing a verbal double take.

'I'm sorry,' I said in a whisper, 'what did you just say?'

The food arrived, and we had to wait while everything was served, ordinary diners enjoying a nice meal out. I stared at my plate, feeling no hunger whatsoever. Nia toyed with hers.

'When Luke fell off that cliff, he was trying to kill me. God, it's at times like this I wish I'd never given up smoking. You always need your props.'

I was so shocked I didn't even think to ask her if this was on the record. Neither did she. She needed no encouragement to tell the whole story. She'd made her mind up, and then she was off with evident relief, even a certain gusto. This is what she said.

'Luke was always a funny child. He had no concentration whatsoever, could never commit to anything. Of course I was to blame for some of it - those weeks away on location, the late, loud nights, and finally the board-

153

ing school in Hampshire while I was away in the States. I knew it at the time I suppose, but paid no heed. I had other things to do then. And he and Stockton never got on.

'When I started to get bored with acting, which had once seemed as important to me as life itself, maybe more so, I started to think more about him, about getting to know him. I got an agent to start looking for a big old place in Mid-Wales. I fondly thought I would be giving something back to the home I'd left all those years before. When I saw the pictures of Glanharan, I fell in love with it straightaway. I had to have it. Stockton was dead against it, but by then I have to admit that I'd ceased caring what he thought. Glanharan would be a fresh start for both of us, for me and Luke.

'He'd always had a determined streak in him. A bit of me, I used to like to think. When he wanted something he had to have it, but once he did have it he usually lost interest. Whatever it was, or whoever, it would be tossed aside and forgotten in an instant.

'At first, when we got to Glanharan, things went better than I could have dreamed. He took to it so well, and he met you, his first real friend, I think.'

'I used to wonder why he didn't seem to have any friends,' I said.

'Please, Glyn, don't interrupt. This is difficult enough for me as it is.'

She put her knife and fork down on her plate, her food barely touched. She took a large swig of wine.

'Then he met Sian. I loved her from the start. I couldn't have been happier. Still drank too much of course, but old habits die hard. There was something about her. Luke felt it, and clearly you did too. Oh yes, I'm afraid it was obvious to me then, maybe not to others. I told Luke he'd have to get in quick. I gave him every encouragement. They seemed so natural together. Everyone said so. And for the first time in his young life, I saw him begin to care about people.

'So that time before the party was the happiest of my life. I know it didn't seem like it sometimes. I, who had got bored with all the endless showbiz parties, now had something to plan for, something to celebrate, something real. Luke told me he wanted to make a little speech that night. Of course I realised straight away what he'd be announcing - how did he think I wouldn't? I was thrilled. I thought she'd be the making of him.

'Everything seemed to be falling into place at last. Slowly, but I believe surely, I was being accepted by the natives, at least that's how it felt. Even your mother, who I could see at once heartily disapproved of me - and I did not blame her - even your mother was coming round to me. And in that way too I was reclaiming just a little bit of my heritage, and coming alive again.

'When I was just starting out in the States I used to think how sophisti-cated it would be to be world-weary, to have done everything, to be bored with everything. When I got there it was hell. Before I came to Glanharan, I'd begun to feel I didn't have a home anywhere. Then I got to thinking that home is where you go back to....

'When they all started to arrive that night, they were all so friendly. I felt I was being forgiven somehow. I was playing a role in a way, of course. I had to. Inside I was on tenterhooks, waiting for Luke and Sian. But I had to keep my poise, play the perfect hostess. I was determined. I even got through it without a drink.

'They were late, do you remember? The last to arrive. Everyone else was there. When the door blew open and I went up to greet them. It was my finest moment. Sian was so beautiful, so elegant with her hair swept up. I

looked at her backless dress as she walked in before me, at her pearl choker, and then I noticed something above the choker. A kind of patch. What
was it? Dirt? It couldn't be.... I couldn't quite make it out. I walked quickly behind her to get a closer look. The room was empty now save Sian and
me. I wasn't aware of anyone else. There was no mistaking it, it was a
mole. A mole in the shape of a heart. I'd seen that heart-shaped mole once
before, many years before, just before the war, just before I left Wales, and
I'd never forgotten it. It was on the neck of a new-born baby.'

She stopped to take another swig.

'*My* new-born baby. I recognised it at once. Knew Sian was the baby I'd
given up years before. Oh, I admit I was no angel back then, or indeed
ever. But I was also foolish and selfish, determined to go my own way,
sparing not a thought for the future. I'm afraid I can't say hand on heart
who the father was. As your mother doubtless remembered, I was a bit of a
wild teen. Your generation seems to think sex was invented in the '60s, but
we had our fair share of it in the '30s. I had more than my fair share, I'm
bound to say. All bad boys. So I wasn't interested in who the father was.
Didn't want to be tied down, wanted to be off to make my own way in the
world.

'In those days, in that neck of the woods, there was no such thing as
adoption, or if there was no-one told me about it. Abortion was out of the
question, as my mother made quite clear. And I myself had no idea how to
go about it. I didn't even have to tell my mother - she could spot these
things a mile off. She said she'd manage things if I promised to tell no-
one, not even my father. Then war came. People went away for all kinds of
reasons, no questions asked. I went to stay with some distant cousins near

Aberystwyth who couldn't have children; they would bring the baby up as their own.

'My mother's plan was that after I had the baby I would go back home. I was the eldest of seven, born in quick succession. There always seemed to be a baby in the house. In those days we didn't have running hot water. We had to heat it in kettles on the fire. So the first job of the day was to gather firewood. After that it was non-stop all day long. We lived on what we had on the farm – chickens, fish, rabbits. My mother wanted me back to help her and to keep house for two old bachelor uncles on a nearby farm. I had different ideas. I left the cousins and took the train to London without a backward glance. I never saw any of my family again. But I always thought about my beautiful little baby, and what I remembered in particular was that heart-shaped birthmark...'

She paused a little. It was hard to tell if she was fighting back tears. I couldn't resist butting in, even though she'd warned me not to.

'But how could you be sure?'

'Oh I just knew. Maybe without realising it I even knew before, somewhere deep down, without knowing it, if you know what I mean. I knew there was some bond, some bond between the three of us.

'As you can imagine I was aghast as soon as I saw that birthmark again. The world changed like that.'

She snapped her fingers. The waiter came over, thinking she wanted him to clear away the plates. We waited for him to do it.

'As soon as I saw it, as Sian walked down into the hall in front of me, I knew I had to stop myself from panicking and think fast, playing the hostess all the while, saying how d'you do, nice to meet you, how lovely of you to come.

'But somehow I had to stop the announcement, and stop the relationship, and kill my dream. I told Luke to come to the study with me, there was something I had to tell him. He was unwilling to go at first, couldn't understand why he had to leave the party. But he knew there was something up.....

'At first I didn't want to tell him why. I just said he'd have to stop seeing Sian, that he had to trust me. He just laughed of course. I can see him now, tossing his hair in that way of his.

'"Why should I?" he said. "Give me one good reason."' Nia did Luke's voice, and got him off to a tee.

'I could see there was no other way out, that I'd have to tell him. Even when I did, he acted in the same defiant way as if he were blocking everything out, mentally filtering any barrier to his desire.

'I screamed at him: "For God's sake, Luke, you can't marry your half-sister. You can't, you can't".

'For the first time in his life I thought he was going to hit me. His face by now was blood-red, veins standing out on his neck. This was getting us nowhere, so I changed tack again.

'"You know you can't win this one, Luke",' I told him slowly, quietly, hoping it would penetrate. "It can't work. I'll tell people. I'll tell Sian. That'll mean the end."

'This finally seemed to hit home. He calmed down and I could see him thinking, sitting there on the desk. He slid off, came towards me. He seemed his old self again.

'"OK Ma," he said. "I'm sorry. It's just a bit of a shock. Just need time to think, that's all, to work things out..."

'"There's nothing to work out, Luke," I said. "You have to accept it."

'"What shall I tell Sian? About the announcement? We were going to announce our engagement just after midnight."

'"Tell her anything. Tell her it's not the right time."'

'He said OK, he'd make a deal. He had to have a little time. We were to go back to the party and he'd work out how to put off the announcement at least, and we'd talk about it again the next day. I said I couldn't possibly just carry on as if nothing had happened. "Oh, come on Ma, it'll be one of your greatest roles". I was so afraid that he just couldn't take in the seriousness of the situation. But he left me little choice. I was a little afraid of him, to tell the truth.

'So we went back to the party and tried to make the most of it, somehow. I don't know what he told her in the end. I could see her looking at me in a puzzled kind of way, but quite unruffled.

'Those hours dragged and dragged. And then when midnight did finally come we had to sing that Godawful song. "Should Auld Acquaintance be Forgot." I've never been able to sing it since.

'Needless to say I did not get any sleep that night. Thank God I'd always kept the rule about separate bedrooms. I kept trying to figure out ways around it, looking at it from different angles, trying to see it as the solution to something and not the problem. But it always came out the same way. Simple. No two ways about it. I had to put a stop to it. I didn't even get round to thinking what I was going to do about Sian.'

She stopped suddenly, as something struck her.

'She doesn't know she was adopted, does she?' It was more of a statement to be confirmed, rather than a question.

'No, I'm pretty sure she doesn't,' I said. 'She'd certainly never mentioned it. Her parents are dead now. Well, her adopted parents.'

'Well, anyway, in the morning there was a desperate tension, which everyone but me and Luke and Sian I suppose put down to dreadful hangovers. But of course there was something else hanging over us.

'I can't remember who suggested the walk up that bloody hill. Sian maybe.'

I knew full well it was Nia herself who suggested it. But I knew better than to interrupt again.

'Maybe he put her up to it. Anyway I didn't know what else to do. I wanted to have another talk with Luke - maybe I'd get a chance to have him to myself on the walk. I couldn't think of any other way of getting him on my own in that houseful of people. I just had to get out, I was desperate. But I had to make him give me his word to break off with Sian, or I'd tell her, I'd made up my mind about that. I thought if I strode out ahead on the walk, he was the most likely to catch me up, young and strong as he was.

'As we were getting to the top, to that path close to the edge, I felt Luke suddenly by my side at last.

'"Careful, Ma," he said, and took my arm. Of course I didn't think......I was just glad that we were to have our little talk.

'But before I had the chance I felt a push, I'm sure I did, but didn't have time to think who or what it was. Before I knew where I was I had my hands round that bush. I looked up and could see Luke stretching towards me through the fog. He had the same face as the night before in the study, eyes and veins bulging. His hand was coming down towards me, but it wasn't stretched out sideways to grasp mine, it was held up flat to push me. Just then I felt something solid under my foot, a little ledge of rock. I put both my feet on it just as he was about to push. As his hand came towards me, I reached up towards him and grabbed his arm, and pulled as hard as I could. It was some survival instinct, stronger than the maternal one, God help me.'

14

I left the restaurant numbed. It was still only just after nine and I needed to go somewhere to think, couldn't face going home yet. You knew I was out for the evening, working. I didn't feel like sitting at a bar by myself so wandered into Soho and went in Caffe Italia for coffee, just down the street from Soho Square. But it was noisy and crowded and I couldn't find a place to sit. It was too cold to sit outside, or even walk around. I couldn't think of anywhere quiet and warm at this time of night. In the end I hailed a cab and told him to drive around for a while, like they do in films. I didn't mind where. The cabbie didn't bat an eyelid and I wondered how often he got asked to do this.

In the cosy anonymity of the back of the cab, the lights and life of the West End whizzing past me. I remembered my first time in a London cab, and tried to marshal my thoughts.

Firstly, I had a new mother-in-law, you had a new mother and Luke had a new grandmother. Secondly, I had a pretty good story on my hands.

Maybe Nia Barry was not exactly hot copy these days, but this confession-al would be good if handled in the right way. Nia hadn't said any of it was off the record. But even though she had blithely or perhaps tactically ig-nored the fact that I was there to do any interview, she made me promise after she told the story: don't tell Sian, at least not yet. I guess that covered the off the record part of it. I began to protest – I'd have to tell you - but she cut me off and that part of her story was clearly at a close. The safest thing to do – it seemed so by mutual assent – was to go through the mo-tions of the press interview: her career, the show, her return to London. It wasn't much of a story after what she'd just told me. When we'd finished she stood up and said we must keep in touch but made no effort to give me her address or telephone number. Then, without so much as a backward glance, she walked out.

I didn't seriously think about writing a story about it - how could I with-out breaking my promise not to tell you? It was a dilemma though, and strangely enough one I hadn't faced before. It's ingrained into journalists that the story is everything, you go after it and get it at no matter what cost. And this wasn't just a case of publish and be damned, it was a case of damning my son's grandmother. But of course it was ridiculous, I would have to tell you. How could I possibly not? What right had Nia to swear me to the silence she had maintained all this time?

Which brings me to the third thing I thought about in that taxi. Was I withholding information if I didn't say anything, breaking some law? I have to admit I was more than a little hazy on this. I was pretty sure that if all the facts had been available at the time Nia would have been subject to questioning by the police, if not actually charged. You can't just yank someone to their death, even in self-defence, without somebody doing something about it, can you? And what about the lapse of time? Did it still count? And space? Once she was back in New York could there be extradition proceedings? Would it be deemed worth the effort?

By this time I noticed the clock was ticking up at an alarming rate so told the driver to take me home to Finchley. When I got in you had a fire burning in the grate and candles burning on the mantelpiece. It was a picture of domestic bliss, the perfect antidote to the turmoil I was feeling inside. But I could tell from your slightly arched eyebrow that you sensed immediately that something was wrong.

'I saw Nia tonight,' I said, after you'd poured us both a glass of wine. 'Interviewed her for this series I'm doing.'

You did not rush me or press me, bless you, although I could see you could barely contain yourself.

'She seems well,' I said, my words seeming all the more bland after her revelations, the revelations I could not reveal. 'Keen to hear all about you. And Luke.'

You smiled sorrowfully, your lips folded in.

'Does she blame herself?'

I shot you an involuntary glance as you sat on the floor by the fire, sipping your wine. You always did have a way of cutting to the quick of things, but I couldn't tell how much you understood. And when it came to it, somehow I just couldn't bring myself to tell you. Something was holding me back.

'I don't think so,' I said slowly.

'So what are you going to say?'

'Say?'

'Say about her in your piece for the paper?'

I wasn't prepared for that one.

'Actually I don't think it'll make a piece. She's made a new life for herself, put it all behind her, leads quite a quiet life I think.'

You seemed disappointed.

'So will you see her again?'

'I really don't know,' I said.

In the event I told Jo that Nia wouldn't make a feature after all, that she hadn't had much to say. I quickly found some old ham to make up the series of five, and bashed out some bog standard stuff. It was a sorry end to what was quite a good series. Jo herself said as much.

That Christmas we'd planned to stay in the flat in Glanharan, which we'd bought a few months before. We'd spend Christmas day with Alun and his family, my mother and father and Tom at Bryngwanwyn. I always looked forward to these trips back home with a tiny amount of trepidation. At least this year we'd have our own retreat, although I still felt just a small pang of guilt of owning a second home. It was what other people did, not us. As a youngster I disapproved of the holiday home industry in Wales which damaged village life with high property prices and houses empty for most of the year, but I didn't go quite so far as to approve of the people who burnt them down.

As we piled into the car in the customary flap on Christmas Eve morning I was hit by a new challenge. So far you had accepted my low-key account of meeting Nia after all those years, but what, if anything, would I say to my mother? I'd never been able to keep much from her. And I'd never got to the bottom of her hostility to Nia, even though Nia had said in The Ivy that she herself understood it. Surely it couldn't just be because she had an illegitimate baby?

We crawled through the northern sprawl of the city and the motorway traffic was heavy across the southern English flatlands, and as we began to see Welsh hills I found myself picking up, thinking it would be alright. When we crossed into Mid-Wales by Trewern I was struck by the strong silvery light which streamed through the clouds like searchlights and shined up the River Severn, the twisting road ahead and even the telegraph wires. The weak, watery sun was fierce in its reflection. In the distance the hills faded into the misty horizon - the sight I missed most. I always forgot how much more dramatic the weather was in Wales, probably because of the hills, I don't know, how sun and cloud combined to give unusual lighting effects. On the one or two visits Mam had paid since we lived in London, she used to complain that there was 'no weather' there.

I caught myself looking at Luke in the mirror. I'd been doing this quite a bit since I saw Nia, probably trying to detect something of her in him, or even something of his namesake uncle. Sometimes I found myself worrying about character traits too. After all, his uncle had tried to kill his grandmother and his grandmother did kill his uncle. But that way madness lay.

I could see his eyes, shining like the river, those eyes I remembered when he was just a few weeks old, fixated by a light when I was trying to rock him to sleep, and his eyes kept rolling backwards as he struggled to keep awake. Those trusting eyes are what I remember and his skin, so fresh and clear. I would wrap in him in my arms and feel we needed each other in equal measure. Those eyes were still the same, but now full of challenge and adventure. I was glad to see the spirit in his eyes. No, I could certainly see nothing of his dead uncle in him.

I could sense you watching me watching him and I glanced across at you and you were. You smiled. Again I wondered if you knew more than you were letting on.

We entered the Haran valley and on the left I could just make out the huge hulk of Bryn Grwnan, swathed in swirling cloud. Since that day, the day of Luke's death, it had always had a mournful air for me, but now was invested in something more, something sinister. Seeing it made me feel slightly sick. We passed through the village and swung right, crunching up the gravelly drive to Glanharan. It's funny how a place can change so completely yet stay the same, lose its mystique of another age. Its manicured lawns, shorn of shrubs, were so different now, and I could see that the trees in the dell which led up to Bryngwanwyn had also been thinned out and the brook filled in and flattened as it approached Glanharan, so you could now just catch a glimpse of the slate roof of the farmhouse beyond the hill. The Glanharan I knew was no longer there, just a big red-brick building divided up into flats. Shiny new silver cars were parked outside on an enlarged, gravelled forecourt.

We took our bags from the car and opened the front door where you and Luke had made your last entrance together all those years ago. You hesitated in the doorway for just one beat, looking up and around. I wondered if, like me, you could almost hear ghostly echoes of that jazz band. We climbed up the vast wooden front stairs to the flat overlooking the lawn above Nia's old room. I could barely think it was the same place, yet flashes came back at the twist of the stairs where parallel universes met.

The flat was small but we'd made it bright and cosy. We weren't long straightening ourselves out and you said you'd drive into the village to gather supplies with Luke and I said I'd walk up the hill to see my parents.

167

It was odd walking up the path again after all that time, as if somehow I shouldn't be there.

When I got to the bungalow my mother was in the kitchen dusting warm mince pies with icing sugar. She wiped her hands on her pinny and hugged me, her smile softened by the years and if I didn't know her better I'd swear there was a small tear in her left eye.

'Good to see you, boy,' she said, holding on to me a bit longer than usual, then went back to her job.

'Where's Dad?'

'Oh he's out down the garden somewhere", she said, as if he were something she continually mislaid. 'And where's that grandson of mine?'

'Gone to the shops with his mother. You'll see him tomorrow. Shall we have a little drink as it's Christmas Eve?'

I glanced through the window and could see my father waddling down the garden path, finding God knows what do out there at that time of year. It was that old familiar gait which all farmers have, swaying slightly from side to side. My mother has it too. When I was young I put it down to the fact that she had to carry buckets of water up from the well, before we were on the water mains. A colleague of mine on the paper came originally from a farm in Uruguay, and I remembered her telling me once that when she first came to Britain she went to the Scottish Highlands and stayed at a farm that did Bed and Breakfast. When she first saw the farmer walking up the yard she had the absurd thought that it was her father; they walked in exactly the same way. People are the same the world over, really.

I poured my mother a sherry and myself a whisky, and once the mince pie dusting was done, managed to get her out of the kitchen to sit down for a chat. I looked around the room, strange and familiar at the same time, with some old heavy pieces from the farm, too big for this new room. The smell was the same too, that unmistakable smell of Bryngwanwyn kitchen, tangible, comforting. I could never pin it down exactly, what constituted that smell. Carbolic soap was in there somewhere.

After we caught up on all the news I plunged in.

'I saw Nia Barry a few weeks ago. She's in London doing a play.'

'Oh yes?" said Mam, looking out of the window.

'You never really approved of her, did you?'

She sipped her sherry.

'No, I didn't.'

'Why not?'

'You have to realise, Glyn, how things were in those days. Remember I came from up country like she did. I knew the people, I knew the gossip... She was what we considered a bad lot, always making trouble, never fitting in.'

She paused and sat there twiddling her glass.

'How is she now?'

'She's fine. Living in a flat in New York, doing the odd bit of work to tide her over.'

I found this was the best way to get my mother to speak, to give her little scraps of information so she'd want more. There was silence for a while, apart from the ticking of the grandfather clock.

'Do you think she ever got over her son's death?' she asked. It was odd. She seemed sort of..... nervous.

'I don't think you ever fully get over something like that, do you? I think whatever happened in her life she's had to come to terms with, make her peace.'

'Well, I guess I wish her that too.'

'What exactly did you know about her? What was the gossip you mentioned?''

'I knew she had a baby when she shouldn't.'

So she had known all along. Could it possibly have made a difference if we'd had this talk years ago? Probably not.

I feigned a surprised, inquisitive look.

'Everybody knew it. They always did, no matter what lengths people went to shut it all up.'

'And you blamed her?'

'Of course we blamed her. She came from a good, hard-working family. They must have asked themselves where they went wrong.'

'But she wasn't the only one?'

'Oh no, she wasn't the only one. But not many would walk away from their child completely, without ever looking back. Nia Barry just ran. Even animals look after their young.'

So that was it. Not just that Nia had had a baby, but that she'd left it.

'And now, do you blame her still?'

She took another prim sip of her sherry and passed her tongue across her lips.

'Well, things are a bit different now. You see all sorts. You don't blame or judge people like you used to. Perhaps that was wrong.'

She seemed to have decided at last to make a clean breast of everything.

'Perhaps there was some jealousy there. She managed to get away, to make her own life. The rest of us had to stay behind and get on with it, live the lives we were born to.'

'But that's exactly what made her have to give the baby up – the gossip, the judgements.'

'She should have found a way.'

I felt we were at last talking as equals, some of that distance between us was being bridged. Maybe she felt the same. She gave me an odd look.

'There's something else. Something I never told you. Maybe I should have.' She stopped.

'Well, what?'

'You had an uncle you never knew about. My brother Jack. He hung himself from an apple tree when he was seventeen. The rumour was, well, that he was the father of Nia's child.'

'Good God. Why didn't you ever tell me?'

'Nain wanted it that way. It upset her just to hear his name. So we never spoke about him.'

'So he was just blotted out of the family? But I've seen photos. He wasn't in them.'

'I know, it seems strange now. He was older than the rest of us. I was about nine or ten at the time. I think Nain must have burnt all the photographs with him in. After she died I found just one of him in her bedside drawer. You look a bit like him. Remember after she had the stroke, she kept saying that you'd come back? I think she thought you were Jack.'

'Did she know about Nia?' *did remember, but at the time put it down to her stroke, as Mam suggested.*

'No, I've thought about that. I don't think she can have. Otherwise she would never have been so polite to her when she came to Bryngwanwyn. We never spoke about it, of course. I heard it from kids in the playground. Kids can be so cruel. They repeated what they heard their parents saying. But maybe no-one said it to Nain's face.'

Odd to be mistaken for someone you never knew. It weighed down my heart with a strange sadness.

171

I was suddenly struck by the full import of what Mam and said.

'But that would mean......?'

I was going to say that that would mean that you were my cousin. But then Mam didn't know that you were Nia's daughter. It was OK to marry your cousin wasn't it? But wasn't there some risk if cousins had children, making any genetic weaknesses more pronounced? I vaguely remembered Mam saying something of the sort once about some cousins she knew who'd married. But of course I couldn't ask her.

'What would that mean?' asked Mam.

My thoughts raced.

'Did he leave a note?'

'Yes. It just said, "Forgive me".'

'So you didn't know for sure? You didn't know for sure that he was the father of the child, or that that's why he killed himself?'

'Not for sure, no. But that's what everyone said. They must have had a reason. No smoke without fire, as they say. He knew what they were saying too. In the end he just couldn't take any more of the gossip, the dirty looks. There was no other reason why he should have done what he did.'

'But, Mam, there *is* smoke without fire. If Nia was such a bad lot, as you say, it could have been, well, it could have been any number of people?'

'But Jack was the one who hung himself.'

'And do you know what happened to the baby?' I asked, a little hoarsely.

'No, that I never did.'

The kitchen door burst open with my father leaning against the frame, exhausted from whatever he had been doing, sweating, his trousers hitched up to the top of his belly and tied around with baler twine. Old habits die hard.

'Where's the boy?" he asked, looking at us both, sensing perhaps that something had passed between us.

I found it hard to concentrate, make normal conversation.

'Gone into Llanfair with his mother,' I said. 'He'll be up tomorrow.'

'Bit early in the day, isn't it, Nell?' nodding at her glass and winking at me. 'Suppose I'd better join you.'

As I was leaving Mam came with me to the door.

'If you talk to Nia again, pass on my best wishes. She can't have had an easy life.'

I mulled over what Mam had said. I had to find out if my Uncle Jack was your father. And there was only one person who could tell me. Nia.

15

Christmas passed pleasantly enough, even merrily. I managed to suspend my anxieties about Uncle Jack and Nia and enjoy the moment, but at times I caught myself looking anxiously at Luke checking for any unspecified flaws. He seemed his usual cheerful self.

We all spent Christmas Day in the farmhouse kitchen talking over old times, or some of them. The old kitchen had also had a make-over, as it would be termed these days. Tiles had replaced the old flagstones, kitchen units lined the walls where the huge old dresser used to stand, and there was a bright red Aga instead of the old black range. But I could still hear echoes of the old kitchen and its tales.

Dad was at his best, telling stories of local characters - he was a great mimic. One of his favourite themes was wartime and the Home Guard, or Dad's Army as everyone now called it. Each character from the TV show had an equivalent in his unit, it seemed. He'd be wheezing with laughter so much that he couldn't finish the story, but everyone knew them well enough by now so we could all join in. I marvelled each time how much fun could be had, or at least recalled, from the darkest of days. It was a good family Christmas, with just enough snow outside to be white but not enough to get in anyone's way too much. Luke in particular seemed to enjoy it. Once or twice you caught me looking at you, trying to see if I could discern any family resemblance, any sign that you could be the daughter of Uncle Jack and Nia. You returned a questioning look. I smiled. I remembered those looks we exchanged at Nia's New Year's Party. Family secrets. And while I thought that Luke's behaviour was strange then, I was now in a very similar position.

We left feeling refreshed and ready for London again. But on the way back in the car, my thoughts turned to Nia, even though I promised myself I wouldn't think about it for a while. There were more questions now, and even though I wanted so badly to talk it over with you, reasons not to began to pile up in my head. You had loved your parents, we'd all had good times with them and Luke had been very fond of them. Was it my place to interfere with that? And all I would be offering her was a mother who didn't acknowledge her or her son, and a father who committed suicide. That must have been when a certain gulf started to open up between us.

I fully intended to get in touch with Nia straightaway, but somehow when I was back in the rhythm at work I kept putting it off. January was traditionally a dull month in Fleet Street, with even some of the most seasoned drinkers dried out after the Christmas excess. Our local, universally known as The Stab - short for The Stab in the Back as it was where editors took hacks to sack them - was almost empty every night.

Even so I couldn't quite summon up the energy to get in touch with Nia, until you challenged me that time. You suggested a quiet Friday night at our favourite Turkish restaurant across the road. Luke was at a sleepover, as they had begun to call them.

'Glyn, I know there's something up,' you said as we got stuck into our hot mezze. 'God knows I've been patient, put it down to the stresses of Christmas and work and so on, but enough's enough.'

I fumbled around looking for an excuse that you might just accept, at least for the time being, but knew before I began I wouldn't succeed.

'Look unless you tell me, I'll be imagining all kinds of dreadful things. I'll begin to suspect you're having an affair,' you said with a mischievous, smiling question mark on your face but I could tell you were half serious. It was true that a gulf that had opened up between us seemed to be widening by the day. If I didn't do something about it, it could only get bigger.

Damn Nia!

So I did tell you - part of it. I said Nia had told me that she had had a baby years ago and had it adopted. I'd mentioned it to my mother at Christmas and she told me the gossip about my uncle being the father. I didn't mention the suicide.

'But why didn't you tell me?' you asked, not unreasonably.

'Nia made me promise not to,' I said. 'I only mentioned it to my mother because I always knew she was hostile to Nia and I wanted to know if that was the reason'

'And was it?'

'Yes, it was.'

'What happened to the baby?'

'No-one knows.'

I could tell you were highly offended.

'But, Glyn, we've never had secrets from each other. Why start now? It could only lead to trouble.'

'I was just trying to respect Nia's wishes.'

'So you put Nia before me?'

'No, Sian. It's not like that and you know it isn't.'

You weren't mollified. Things were rather frosty between us for the rest of the evening.

Next day I wrote to Nia from the office on headed paper so she'd reply there and you wouldn't see the envelope. I asked all the questions that had being swimming round in my head going nowhere, and asked her outright if Jack Davies was your father. I also said that I was keeping my promise to her not to tell you who your mother was, but it was putting a strain on our relationship and you were beginning to suspect all sorts of things. I passed on my mother's good wishes.

I didn't know if I was really expecting a reply and didn't get one for several weeks. I was just thinking about getting on the phone to her agent but one morning spotted a handwritten cream envelope with a New York postmark sitting on top of the pile on my desk. I couldn't remember if I had ever seen Nia's handwriting but thought I couldn't have as I would have recognised it at once: strong, sloping, old-fashioned American.

It was a rambling and rather maudlin letter, in places repetitive and in others contradictory. It was on her own notepaper, her address - an Upper East Side apartment - and telephone number printed on the top right. It had clearly taken a great deal of writing. I found it interesting to see what she responded to first. I still have the letter in the top drawer of my desk at work, and this is what it says.

Dear Glyn,

How sweet of you to write. It meant so much to me to hear the kind words from your mother. It's almost as if my own family have forgiven me, although it's too late for that. Well, not forgiven, but at least understood a little. Perhaps it's the same thing. Age mellows you, if you've had a good and lucky life, and helps you look back on the past and put it all in perspective. What really matters is to recognise the good you have and hold on to it as hard as you can.

Forgive my tardiness in replying. I've found strength in silence over the years, as I'm sure you understand, and it's a hard habit to break. But I've also learnt that what I used to consider my strengths, or some of them, now seem to be my weaknesses, and vice-versa. So I look for strength in the weaknesses of others wherever I can. Perhaps that's one of life's greatest lessons.

I can't really remember exactly what I told you in The Ivy, other than the bare facts, of course, but I can tell you that Jack Davies Gwylym *was not the father. I'd forgotten that he was your mother's brother. We never consummated the relationship, if that's what you can call it. He wanted to of course, but by then I was already pregnant. When he found out, he offered to marry me, but I was having none of it. He was a nice boy. It hit me hard when he killed himself. I can only hope that it wasn't because of me.*

Thinking back, when I came to Glanharan I was aware of the connection in a vague way, aware too of your mother's enmity towards me and couldn't blame her. I could really do nothing to reach out to her, save try-

ing all the wiles I knew, but then of course I should have known that they would be wasted on her. Your family always showed uncommon sense.

We came from the same stock, your mother and I. I felt I knew her instinctively, and she me. But this common origin and our later very different lives, with you in between if you know what I mean, made it all but impossible to connect.

You ask, not in so many words because you're too polite and well brought-up, why I came to Glanharan in the first place. Hindsight puts a different imperative on these questions, but I suppose in my own mind at the time I wasn't really going back, not to that part of Wales which held for me such miserable memories, to which I would never want to return, never even wanted to visit when I was there. I was going there on my own terms.

Psychologically, I suppose, now you hear so much more of that sort of thing, I wanted to face my own demons, although I would never have framed it so, even to myself. I guess I have to admit I believed it was my next big role, for such had been my understanding of goals and success in my life until then. My third act.

When I was at Glanharan I began to feel for the first time something of a celebrity, something I never really did before, or maybe just a bit when I got my first couple of leads, but then it was all B stuff - major roles in minor movies. In the States that adds up to nothing, in Aberharan it made me a star. And I began to enjoy it in a way, because I had something to show off - Luke, and then Sian.

I'd left my home years before, such as it was, to make my fame and fortune but pretty soon I realised the journey was more satisfying than the destination - I'd got fed up before I quite got there. Maybe you're wondering if my career was going nowhere anyway. I was doing alright, just

179

bored with the whole damn shooting match. I'd also begun to feel guilty for having put my career before Luke, and for abandoning Sian. Maybe somewhere in the back of my mind I might even have thought I might find her, but I hardly admitted that to myself.

I suppose I did worry about giving up my status, my importance. But it's only you yourself who worries about status. Most people worth bothering about take you for who you are, not what you do. I was lucky enough to realise that. It pays not to take yourself too seriously. No-one else does.

There's a lot to be said for not quite making it to the top of the pile, for what is left when you do? What do you dream about when your dreams come true? And in these days of microwaved celebrity there's a trick too in achieving something on the quiet. I've always admired those people whom I often seem to have played who are not in the full glare of the footlights or floodlights but unobtrusively get on with it and achieve something rather glorious. Fame isn't important, although many of us chase it. It usually goes wrong, or evaporates, and then we're left looking around us for the important things in life we missed.

So although my career was hardly illustrious I was quite content to hang up my hat and come home. Because despite everything I did think of it as home. Of all the definitions of home I've heard, the one I like the best is: home is where you go back to. No matter what awaits you there.

And I still don't regret going back, you know. Regret is something I've never had much time for or seen much point in.

But after Luke's death I knew I had to get away immediately and never go back. Stockton and I separated and divorced, Briddy was enjoying new-ly-wedded bliss, and I was alone in my grief and guilt, the only way I could get through it. When the money started running out I started doing *bits and pieces here in the US and made a comfortable enough living. I got by.*

I'm sorry to hear that you and Sian have not being getting along, and that I might have played a part in that. I know you are strong enough to come through it. I beg of you not to tell her anything while I'm still around - that's probably not too long to go. You'll find something to say to her to smooth things over. I just couldn't bear to have old wounds opened up again, Glyn, it would kill me, and it wouldn't do her much good either. I hope you understand that it's for the best. If you don't now, you will in time.

You know I've always had this stubborn streak in me. People used to tell me it was a weakness, and it goes back to what I was saying earlier. Sometimes your weaknesses save you.

I think about you all often, every day. Thank you for the pictures. Luke is a fine boy. He would have made his uncle very proud, and it heartens me immeasurably to know that, somehow, things live on.

Yours ever,

Nia. '

16

I was furious. Relieved about Uncle Jack of course, but I still had the problem of what to do about you, about us. I found Nia's attitude selfish and solipsistic, which may always have been traits of hers, but they had always been tempered by a certain generosity of spirit. How could she feel guilt and no regret? And couldn't she acknowledge that she had a family now, responsibilities? When she wrote 'his uncle' at the end, it was the only acknowledgment of the blood and bonds we all shared.

I tried to concentrate on the good in Nia. She'd introduced me to art and jazz, to wine and fine cuisine. And she'd given me the confidence, I now realised, to be myself, to go out and make my own life. But this just served to make her stance seem all the more unreasonable.

As I mulled it all over, I began to wonder if there was something else, some other secret that made Nia so determined that I shouldn't say anything to you, so stubborn about it. And then, when I was lounging on the sofa one morning over the Sunday papers, I hit upon something that must have been niggling at me in The Ivy. She said that she took us all up to Bryn Grwnan that day so she could get Luke on his own to talk to. In the cold light of day, this seemed a ridiculous explanation. Surely that would have been far easier at Glanharan?

I could still picture her grim determination as she led the way up to the ridge, her air of purpose. Could it be that her original intention had been to push him over? It would have been a quick solution to her dilemma. That would explain it. She wanted to protect you not only from a mother who had abandoned you, but a mother who was a murderess. It was one thing to yank Luke off the mountain in self-defence, another to take him up there meaning to kill him.

My heart was beating. Had I stumbled on what had really happened? You came in from the kitchen and sat on the rug in front of the fire, picking through the papers without much enthusiasm. Your presence calmed me down a little. I was probably making up ridiculous scenarios of my own. And in a curious way, there was a part of me that admired Nia's spirit. I wondered if I myself was being selfish, expecting too much of a woman in her twilight years.

Things hadn't improved between me and you. In fact they'd got worse. We'd got out of the habit of talking through our troubles and were both unhappy, alone. I'd been putting off things, waiting for Nia's reply, hoping for a solution. But I must have been even worse after it came.

Luke of course felt it too, and one night he came into my study where I was working on some feature or other, a glass of Laphraoig on my desk. It's the old roll-top that Nia brought to Glanharan. I bought it when the contents were auctioned off.

Luke hardly ever came in when I was working, so I knew he wanted to talk about something, but he didn't come to it straight away. He ambled around in that distracted, distant air of one of his age, picking up a couple of objects he couldn't possibly be interested in and making painful attempts at conversation.

'Has anything changed between you and Mum?' he mumbled eventually. It was a good question, I thought, one you couldn't easily dodge, one which deserved a good answer. I'm sorry to say I didn't give him one.

'Why, do we seem different?'

'You don't seem to have as much fun any more. And neither do I.'

'Well, I suppose everyone goes through patches when they don't get on so well.'

He waited patiently for something better.

'I probably haven't been talking to her enough lately. I've been a bit busy with work.'

'But work's the same as usual, isn't it? What's new?'

He was digging right in there, I'd say that for him.

'Maybe you're right, maybe I should make more of an effort.'

'Good,' he said, and got up to go.

'Luke,' I said as he was turning the door handle.

'What?'

'Thanks,' I said with a smile. He didn't smile back.

'Just do it, Dad.'

I could see now that it was time for action. I'd been thinking about writing back to Nia, or even phoning her, and begging her to reconsider, but really I knew there was no point.

What could I say to you though? I ran quickly through the options that night in my study. It was out of the question even to hint that Nia was your mother, and I also ruled out the story of Luke's death - one didn't make sense without the other. Maybe I should have stood up to Nia, not have made the ridiculous promise. But maybe I was making this too complicated.

We went to the Turkish restaurant on Finchley Road, like we used to when we wanted to chat. You would take it as a signal, I thought. It was a good place to go for that, relaxed and lively at the same time. It was always full but you never had to book, indeed they didn't take bookings. They knew us but never made too much fuss. And the house red which they brought in carafes was fine so you didn't even have to trouble over the wine list. When we'd eaten and were enjoying a cigarette I took a deep breath.

'Look, I'm sorry I've been a bit of a miserable bastard recently,' I said. 'Or even more of one than usual,' I added before you could.

You sat there, as Luke had, waiting for more but looking interested and receptive.

'When I went to see Nia, it upset me a bit more than I let on, to tell the truth. She feels guilty over Luke's death. It sort of got to me in a way I can't explain. I've written to her, asking her to explain more, but she'll only go so far.'

'I do understand,' you said. 'I don't expect you to tell me all the details. But it's when you don't tell me things - just simple things like writing to her - that we're bound to drift apart a little. I resent it, and resent myself for resenting it, and you resent me for resenting it, and round and round it goes.'

You suggested brandies, something we very rarely had.

'All I know is, you haven't been right since you saw Nia. If she's confided in you even a little then I'm sure it's done her a power of good to unburden herself. You don't have to tell me her secrets.'

The evening did clear the air a little, and I realised a little belatedly I was silly not to trust you, resorting to writing in secret and making it all worse. But it was temporary. Something fundamental had changed. We started bickering over the smallest things, something we'd never done before. I was probably irritable, locked in my secret anger with Nia. You even went to stay with your friend Anna for a few days, saying you needed a break.

'What about Luke?' I said.

'His father will look after him,' you said.

That shook me up a bit. I didn't realise that things were so bad for you – that I was so bad for you. It was very unlike you to leave Luke like that. I dreaded that you wouldn't come back. I phoned, promising I'd change, make more of an effort, go to counselling, whatever it took.

And I wrote to Nia. I told her how annoyed I was that you and I, and even Luke, had to go through this because of her. That you had left me. It was good to get it off my chest. You did come back, and once again I tried to put the whole Nia thing out of my mind, to concentrate on us.

I didn't hear anything from Nia for a few weeks, and almost managed to put the whole thing behind me. Then I got a scribbled, unrepentant note, saying she knew we'd find a way. After that our correspondence dwindled to the odd postcard and Christmas card, addressed to all of us now, at home. In time you and I patched things up and got on with our lives, but somehow things were never quite the same. Inside me there was still anger and disappointment that Nia refused so cold-bloodedly to acknowledge her new-found family and shirked the consequences of her past life.

I still thought about her often, and as the years passed grew less bitter about her determination not to face the present.

Then a couple of years ago, I found myself in New York for a few days on a story. I'd taken her number with me and told you I might give her a ring.

'She may finally lay old bones to rest,' I said without much hope. You encouraged me to go and see her.

'She'll be about eighty now,' you said. 'Maybe she'll see things differently.'

Suddenly I decided on a new tack. I'd put my foot down and tell Nia I could no longer keep it all from you, that it was unfair. I'd stand up to her. She and Luke had this in common: somehow I found it difficult to stand up to either of them. Once I'd hit on this course of action, I felt immense relief, as if I'd been released from a great burden. It seemed the obvious thing to do, and I didn't know why I hadn't done it sooner. You noticed the difference in me almost immediately. You said you thought the old Glyn had come back to you.

I waited until the job in New York was almost done before I rang, not knowing quite what to expect, not having heard from her since the Christmas card several months before. It was answered quickly, and there she was on the other end of the line, sounding a little frailer but quite with it.

'Ah, Glyn,' she said, with her old trick of sounding as if she'd seen you a few hours ago. 'What a pleasant surprise.'

She was quite willing to meet me and suggested an early supper the next evening at Sardi's, the theatre restaurant on 42nd St. 'I'll book.'

She was sitting there when I went in, in the corner below the rows and rows of black and white pictures of actors, nursing a martini with a small silver onion in it. I found myself wondering if her picture was there somewhere. If it was, she was not sitting near it.

Her hair was quite white now, still short and styled, her face lined and a little puffed. She was hunched on the banquette, but her eyes still sparkled.

I took the wine menu from the waiter and ordered a bottle of Gamay. Nia laughed.

'I remember the time when you wouldn't know Gamay from scrumpy.'

'Does that make me a better person?'

'No,' she said, unsmiling now. 'No, of course not.'

I showed her the photos I'd brought with me and as Nia pored over them fondly I told her all the news. You were well and we'd patched up our differences, were probably even stronger than before. Luke was fine, seventeen and monosyllabic. My dad had died six months before, but Mam was still there in her bungalow at the bottom of the lane.

'I know you disagree with the way I've gone about things, Glyn, that you're disappointed I didn't embrace you and Sian and Luke.'

I knew it was pointless to protest.

'But it wouldn't have worked, trust me. I'd given just about all the explanations I had. I just couldn't face justifying myself all over again.'

She was in a talkative mood.

'After I moved away from Glanharan there were times when I felt so low that I did think of ending it all. I didn't tell you that before because I was too proud. I couldn't see my way forward for a long while. I passed to that place where death was preferable to life. Couldn't get out of bed in the morning. Ha! I know what you're thinking. I never could. But this was different. I just couldn't see any point. I'd always believed everyone has to find their own meaning in life, and up till then mine had been to have a helluva good time. I couldn't do that any more though. I had to find something else.

'But it was hard. These feelings take control of you, you can't just shake them off. I kept telling myself that it was no ending really, going out at your lowest ebb, at the worst point of your life. And I couldn't help but realise that it was that spark of the life force that caused it all in the first place, that made me reach up to that hand and pull it, that survival instinct.

'Well, gradually I found bits of work and found some sort of rhythm that could keep me going. That's all we have in the end - work. All the greats say it: Voltaire, Chekov. But I had to steel myself to it. You can't imagine the roles I had cast for myself - Medea, Magda Goebbels. Or perhaps you can. And when I found out you had Sian and Luke, I couldn't change course again. When you've been to rock bottom you can find a sort of still serenity if you manage to bounce back up. And that's what I had to settle for. I didn't mind growing older but I did mind losing a sense of adventure, of passing from adventurer to survivor.'

'But we would have loved to have you as part of our family.' I said. 'That could have made such a difference to your life. There've been a good many years. You could have seen Luke grow up.'

I had to give it to her straight, at last.

'No, I would have brought more troubles into your lives. Believe you me. You were better off without me, and I've been better off alone. I'm not a good person to know, Glyn. I bring trouble into people's lives. I didn't want to bring it into yours. What you tell them when I'm dead and gone is up to you.'

'I'm not reproaching you, Nia. I'm telling you that you are loved, and that you have a family whether you like it or not. You're not a bad person, and you're wrong to think it. Yes, you've met tragedy, but you can't blame yourself.'

Or could she? The question of her real purpose in taking us up the mountain was on my mind. It was now or never.

'There is one thing I want to ask you, Nia.'

'Well, shoot. I'll answer it truthfully. I owe you that.'

'You said that you took us up Bryn Grwnan so you could get Luke on his own to talk. Did you have any other reason?'

Nia looked at me squarely and smiled a sad little smile, as if to say 'How clever of you to have worked that out.' She knew straightaway what I meant.

'It had crossed my mind, that if I did manage to get him on his own, I could threaten to push him off if he wouldn't promise to give up Sian. I wanted him to see how serious I was about it. I wouldn't have done it of course – apart from anything else he was so much stronger than me. I was desperate, but not that desperate. But when I did see him lunge at me with hatred in his eyes, it was as if that thought helped me do it. It was him or me.'

I believed her. She was needlessly straightening her cutlery.

'When I was a little girl, my best friend was my Auntie Wyn. She was in her nineties and lived alone in the same little cottage she'd moved to when she was married. It was the kind of life I never wanted but something drew me to her.

190

'She wasn't my real auntie of course. My grandmother's sister, I think. Things always seemed to be mixed up back then. You'd call people Auntie who weren't and you'd call your real uncle by their first name.

'Her husband had been the village undertaker and she was the midwife. The hatcher and dispatcher they used to call them. Seeing so much of life from both ends, she was a wise old soul. Her two daughters married and moved away, and she was left alone, and happy with it.

'She somehow knew I'd leave as soon as I could. Our farm was high on a hill overlooking the railway line. As far back as I can remember I used to look at the clouds of steam snaking through the valley, next stop London as I had it in my mind, and knew I would be on it one day with a one-way ticket.

'It wasn't that my parents weren't good. They were. I'm sure your mother told you. Perhaps too good. Perhaps it was me that wasn't good, that didn't fit.

'So I knew my life lay elsewhere, that if I didn't go I would be a disappointment to them. And to myself. I was about ready to go when I found I was pregnant with Sian. Auntie Wyn knew about that too, I'm sure, and must have sorted things out with my mother and the cousins.

'Afterwards, when I made my mind up to go and tell no-one, I went down to see her on my bike. I'd cut some flowers from the garden and put them in the saddlebag on the back, their heads jutting out. Of course I went down the hill too fast and fell off, but didn't notice that all the heads had broken off so when I went to present them to her they were just a bunch of stalks.

'I don't think I've ever heard anyone laugh so much since, let alone anyone over ninety.

'She made us tea, and then asked, "Has anyone ever told you you need a great deal of courage to get through life?"

'I said no, not really knowing what she was on about.

'"Well you do," she said, "a great deal of courage."

'She left it at that. And oddly enough, although I didn't give those words a second thought at the time, they've stayed with me. At times when I've needed it, they've come back to me. Life does take a lot of courage, and you're better off for knowing it. That was the last time I saw her. We said cheery goodbyes as we usually did. She'd insist on hobbling out to the gate to see me off, waving. She died a few months later. And I never spoke to any of my family ever again.'

She took another large glug of wine – she could still sink it – and started humming a tune which sounded vaguely familiar.

'Do you know where that's from, Glyn?'

'No. I was just trying to place it.'

'It's an aria from a little known opera by Umberto Giordano: *Andrea Chenier.* Callas sang it. I've always loved it. Tom Hanks played it to Denzil Washington in *Philadelphia.* 'I bring misfortune to all who love me,' she sings. That's true of me too. I can't risk entering your lives.'

'But that's not true, Nia,' I said, and meant it.

'Oh, but it is. *La Mamma Morta,* it's called. The dead mother. And that's what I must remain to Sian.'

It was time to let her have it. It was my turn to take a large gulp of wine.

'The thing is Nia, I've made up my mind to tell Sian. I've held out as long as I can. You say you don't want to bring trouble into people's lives, but that's what you've done to ours. This secret has come between us. You more than anyone know what harm secrets can do. You've no right to take

192

this one to your grave. Yes, we've come through it as you said we would, but it's a strain. When I get back to London I'm going to make a clean breast of it and tell her everything.'

There was a silence. Nia wasn't looking at me, but down into her glass. She didn't look angry. She looked kind of.........triumphant.

'There's something else I haven't told you, Glyn. I didn't want to, but now I see I have no option. I'm sick Glyn. I've got this illness with a long Latin name. Or is it Greek? Anyway, basically it means my muscles are going to waste gradually away. It might take years, but eventually I'll be a rag doll. I won't be able to speak, or even swallow.'

'Nia, I'm so sorry.'

'Don't be. It's not going to happen.'

'What do you mean?'

'I'm not going to let it happen. I'm going to Switzerland to that place where they help you die. I've signed up and paid the deposit. And I'm not going to take the secret to my grave. After I've gone you can tell Sian whatever you want – I won't care.'

This certainly took the wind out of my sails. I half-wondered if she was telling the truth, whether this wasn't just a last-gasp ploy to get me to hold my tongue.

'Wh...when will you do that?'

'When things start to get bad. You've got to time it right so that you know there's no longer any hope, but you're not too ill to travel.'

She said it in a matter-of-fact way, as if she were planning a trip to the seaside.

'But how will you manage – getting there, I mean?'

'A friend will come with me. You needn't worry.'

'Briddy?'

'No, Briddy died a couple of years back.'

I wondered who it was. Nia had never spoken of any friends except Briddy.

'You do understand, don't you Glyn?'

I knew the last thing Nia would want were fine words and a bedside manner.

'Not fully, no.' What was the right response to such a question? Judging by Nia's face, that wasn't it.

'But you see, that's why you can't say anything to Sian until after I've gone. Otherwise you'd have to tell her she's adopted, screwed her brother and her mother's about to kill herself. You can't do that to her, Glyn.'

Put like that, I had to agree with her. So Nia would have the last word after all. I searched desperately for something to say, some way of rescuing the evening, but it was over.

We said our goodbyes. They weren't cheery exactly, but Nia maintained a brisk and businesslike air. We had never been good at goodbyes, we just sort of trailed off. This time, I knew I probably wouldn't see her again. She came out of the restaurant on my arm, slowly but steadily. I hailed her a cab, and she was gone.

17

A few days ago, a good ten years after that night in The Ivy, I got a call from Nia's agent, saying she wasn't doing so good and if I was passing through New York could I go and see her.

I wasn't, as it happened, but talked it over with you and we agreed it was the right thing to do to go. I went home, packed a bag and grabbed a few pictures of us and Luke and got the next available flight. I arrived at JFK in the late morning, hired a car and drove across Long Island, which is certainly well named, to Sag Harbour, where Nia was in a nursing home. I enjoyed the journey even on the crowded Long Island Expressway, leaving the dirty sprawl of New York behind me and finding the rolling farmlands with white fences and red barns. It was a blustery, wet February day, and for some reason old phrases from the farm came back to me on the drive. Did you know that this time of year was known as the Cat Days, when cats are on heat and scream their mournful noise of the night? And a lot of rain like this was known as February fill-dyke.

I'm writing this in a pleasant B&B in Sag Harbor, a quaint old-fashioned town on the northern shore of the southern fork of the Island, about three hours' drive from the city. I wonder just how much will come as a surprise. As Nia said, our strengths are sometimes our weaknesses. I thought I was protecting you by doing as she asked, but I was just jeopardising our relationship.

It's late afternoon and when I rang the nursing home they told me to come in the morning, she's always a bit better in the mornings. Makes a change. She always used to say after a heavy night, 'Must go to bed now. Got to be up first thing in the afternoon.'

Sunday seems a suitable day for visiting. I'm toying with the usual kaleidoscope of feelings before seeing Nia, excitement, still a little resentment, sadness too. This will be the last time.

I woke this morning to find a crisp, clear sky with the world underneath washed and dried by yesterday's wind and rain. The breakfast was one of those full-on American affairs where everything that was not fried was drenched in cinnamon. Sag Harbor is almost unnaturally quiet, only the wind soughing through the trees. It looks like one of those Hollywood back lots complete with small-paned shop windows and Victorian lamp-posts.

The home turned out to be a mile or so out of town on the edge of the bay, one of those rambling clapboard jobs with cupolas, a lantern tower and a widow's walk, I think it's called – a kind of balcony on the roof where sailors' wives would look for their men returning from the sea.

It had a massive, glassed-in porch skirting the front. It was here that I found Nia, wrapped in a fringed silk shawl, dozing serenely in a wicker chair loaded with cushions, positioned to look out over the lawns and down at the sea. It was a pleasant space, with plenty of plants and a couple of small chirping birds in a big square white wicker cage that stood on the ground on four legs. But it wasn't exactly warm at this time of year, and Nia was the only one there.

She opened her eyes as I approached and I could see that the sparkle had almost gone, her hair wispy and thin, her skin wrinkled and mottled, a granny grin greeting me. Yet there was still some of her girlishness there, somewhere. Her voice though came as something of a shock. Thin and weak, it came in short bursts between deep laborious breaths.

'Glyn,' she whispered, barely able to hold up a hand, 'how nice of you to come. How long are you here for?'

'Only a day or two. I have to get back to London.'

'Of course. I tire easily these days. But I wanted to see you.'

I told her that you and Luke were well, and Luke was at medical school and going to be a doctor. A ghost of a smile passed over her purple lips.

'A doctor', she repeated, sucking in the word with great satisfaction, as if it was the one word she had wanted me to travel three thousand miles to say.

She looked at me for a long time, and we were both searching for the words.

'The time has come, Glyn. I'm going to Switzerland.'

I was holding her hand, and stared at her in disbelief. It was clear that she was going nowhere, and she herself must know this too.

'It's good to be able to tell someone. I can't talk about it here. They'd try to stop me. But it won't be long.'

Her head lolled back onto the cushions piled up on her chair. Perhaps she needed to cling on to the belief that she still had a choice, that she still had one defiant act of independence left in her.

'I've had a good life, Glyn.'

I was a little taken aback.

'You can say that? Despite everything?'

The question was out before I had a chance to frame it better. But Nia was unperturbed.

'Not despite, because of.'

I didn't quite get what she meant.

'You mean if you had it all over again you'd want it to be like that? Was it all grist to your mill?'

Another unkind question, I reflected as I asked it. But it was time for our last kind of reckoning, when some of my bitterness had to come out. Maybe that's why she wanted to see me.

'I mean that what came along, that's what I had to deal with. There are no ifs. And, yes, you do need battles in life. Sometimes you have to fight them even though you know you can't win. The thing about seeing some tragedy in your life, is that it can make it more precious, somehow. I makes you think you might as well hang on. I know it can go the other way as well. I'm lucky in that way.'

Through the French windows a TV set was blaring, even at this time of the morning, a small cluster of residents, I suppose you'd call them, un-smiling but transfixed. The comfort of nursing homes, I'd once heard TV described. At least the place was clean, and Nia was comfortable.

'There's a Spanish proverb, which says: "Take what you want, but know the price". That way, you can meet death, because you've lived your life.'

She seemed at last to have made some peace with herself, stopped blaming herself. I couldn't help thinking that Luke didn't have the chance to be ready for death, but that was hardly Nia's fault. And he was ready to push her to hers. Then I began to see that Nia had asked me to come, not for her sake, but for mine. For ours.

She must have read the confusion on my face as an inability to handle her readiness for the end.

'Don't worry. I'm ready to go. I'm used to directions. Exit downstage left. Or slow fade to black, as it said on movie scripts. Slow fade to black. I'll settle for that. And then you'll be able to tell my story.'

As her head rolled a little to the side, I could see she was exhausted, looking now very old. I felt guilty, but didn't know why.

'Do you get any visitors?' I asked softly.

She grunted. 'Sal drives out to see me once in a while. My agent. But he's old himself now. And he's a miserable bugger. Don't feel sorry for me Glyn. I'm happy enough. Although God knows this lot could do with some livening up.' She nodded at the crowd in the other room. 'All they ever do is watch TV.'

There was another long pause, broken only by the TV and the chirping birds.

'You'd better go now. Thank you from the bottom of my heart.'

I didn't know what she was thanking me for, but could see she didn't want any more questions. Perhaps I'll never know. But I did know that her determination to live her own life and see it through has to be admired.

I went to give her a peck on the cheek, a little awkwardly with her slumped in the chair, but she managed to thrust her lips on to mine, in that fervent way that old ladies sometimes do with younger men. All words were used up. As I left the conservatory, or porch I suppose Americans would call it, I glanced back, but Nia was already dozing again peacefully.

As I walked down the gravel path, my footsteps crunching in the chill silence, I caught that feeling, that moment, that glimpse of eternity. And my heart gave one of those sudden, immense surges that make you glad to be alive.

Made in the USA
Charleston, SC
26 April 2016